THE
SECRET
—OF—
YELLOW
ISLAND

ABOUT THE AUTHOR

Mary Regan was born on a farm in County Derry but she has spent most of her life in Derry City. She lived for four years in England before returning to Derry where she now teaches in a primary school. Recently she was awarded a Master's Degree from the University of Ulster.

Her interests include folklore, archaeology and drama and she enjoys combining history with a touch of mystery. Donegal is one of her favourite places and she spends her summers in a caravan there. She is married with four children.

THE SECRET OF YELLOW ISLAND

MARY REGAN

POOLBEG

Poolbeg are indebted to Oxford University Press
for their kind permission to reproduce lines from
The Night Sees Ireland Desolate
by Aindrais MacMarcuis

First published in 1993 by
Poolbeg,
A division of Poolbeg Enterprises Ltd,
Knocksedan House,
Swords, Co. Dublin, Ireland.

© Mary Regan 1993

The moral right of the author has been asserted.

Poolbeg receives financial assistance from
The Arts Council of Northern Ireland and
the Arts Council/An Chomhairle Ealaíon, Ireland

A catalogue record for this book is available from the British Library.

ISBN 1 85371 302 3

Cover illustration by Aileen Caffrey
Cover design by Poolbeg Group Services Ltd
Set by Mac Book Limited in Stone 10/14
Printed by The Guernsey Press Limited,
Vale, Guernsey, Channel Islands.

For all my children

Contents

1

Paradise Time

Grannies come in all shapes and sizes—short and fat, tall and skinny, glamorous and cosy—and have all kinds of quirks, but Eimear Kelly knew that there wasn't another in the whole world as dotty as her Nan Sweeney.

"The Sweeneys were never noted for their good sense," Eimear's father was heard to say on more than one occasion. "It's as well for you, my girl, that you also have the Kelly blood in you. A budgie has more wit than your Nan Sweeney."

But Eimear loved her Nan and wished she didn't live so far away. A granny is a great ally when trouble looms and scowling parents have to be soothed.

Summertime was paradise time. Then Eimear would board the rattly bus and head off to Magherabeg to spend two whole months of freedom, fun and being spoilt by her Nan. There was the usual bother trying to get round her father before she could escape but that was all part of the excitement.

"I don't know," he'd grumble to Eimear's mother. "It's time somebody in this family grew up. You're as bad as your mother, and your daughter is heading in the same direction—daft as brushes the lot of you."

Her mother would smile, pat his almost bald head and say, "Sure you love us all the same. Where would you be without the bit of fun and excitement we bring into your life?"

Eimear had to admit that daftness did seem to run on the Sweeney side of the family. Once, when Eimear and her friends were skipping in the street, her mother had appeared out of nowhere and jumped into the rope with the others, chanting, "On the mountain stands a lady/who she is I do not know…"

Another time her mother had sneaked out of the house in the middle of the night when the snow was thick on the ground and had spent a good hour sliding down the hill on a stainless-steel breakfast tray. She thought nobody had seen her but nosy-parker Jane Bell had been watching from her bedroom window and it was all over the school the next day. Parents can be very embarrassing. After her father had grumbled for what he considered a respectable length of time he sighed, ran his hands through what was left of his hair, shrugged his shoulders and said, "I give up. Have your own way. Send her off to that overgrown hippie. But if she turns out like her Nan—don't blame me!"

Magherabeg is a small village that nestles on a small strip of land between the Donegal mountains and the wild Atlantic Ocean. It is a long way from Eimear's home town of Derry and, on a hot sticky day in early July, she was finding the journey tedious. She tried to read but she was too impatient, and instead she passed the time eating everything her mother had packed in her lunchbox.

When they reached the misty boglands and began to climb into the mountains, Eimear knew that she was almost there and excitement bubbled in her stomach. The road was bumpy and she was sorry now she had eaten so much. Unpleasant things were happening to her insides!

The bus lurched round a corner and then hung suspended in mid-air. Hundreds of feet below, the mighty Atlantic churned and pounded on the worn-out rocks, sending jets of white foam high into the air and then sucking them greedily back again. The ocean had carried off great chunks of the land and dropped them out to sea, making a beautiful crumbly, islanded coastline.

Eimear could see Inishbwee—the island her Nan had lived on until she was about nine years of age. It was deserted now. The islanders had grown tired of being cut off for months on end by stormy seas and so, gradually, they had packed up and moved to the mainland. Nan now lived in a cottage just outside the village. Her home snuggled comfortably into a sheltered hollow above a beautiful sandy cove.

Nan, in fact, owned two cottages. They were separated by a rocky, thistly, hillocky field that provided grazing of a sort for her donkey, Oscar. On the morning of her wedding Nan had crossed that field, leaving her family home to start her married life in Granda's cottage. The two cottages had come in handy for they had had eleven children to fill them. Now there was only Nan. Granda had died before

Eimear was born and the children were scattered all over the globe. There were Sweeneys in Tahiti and Borneo, in Zanzibar and Singapore, in Boston and Rio de Janeiro. Only Eimear's mother lived close enough to make regular visits.

Eimear thought about the Farrellys. They were from Belfast and every summer, for as long as she could remember, they had rented Nan's second cottage. At the last count there had been four children in the family—Ronan and Kate and the twins, Brendan and Josie. Kate was ten, the same age as Eimear, and they were special friends. This summer there would be five Farrelly children. Kate had written at Christmas and she was just bursting to tell Eimear about her new baby sister. Although the twins were nuisances at times Eimear, being an only child, enjoyed the rough and tumble of a larger family.

With a screeching protest from the brakes the bus slid to the bottom of the hill and groaned to a halt in front of the post office. Eimear was already on her feet straining to catch a glimpse of her Nan. But there was no need to strain. Nan Sweeney was waiting and nobody with an eye in her head at all could possibly miss her.

She was a sight to see, perched high on her donkey cart and waving furiously. The body of the cart was painted the brightest yellow that ever came out of a tin. The spokes of the wheels were a brilliant scarlet and the rims glittered shiny-black. A riot of painted flowers decorated the sides of the cart and twisted down the shafts towards Oscar, who was brushed to a glossy sheen and sported his best burnished brass and polished leather.

Nan Sweeney herself was the star of the show. Nan

loved dressing up but she wasn't bothered about up-to-the-minute fashions. Her dress was a leftover from the dancing days of her girlhood. It flowed in swirls of pink and purple flowered net around her small, sturdy figure. Around her shoulders was a crocheted cape worked in the finest silver thread. It was Nan's own work and it almost covered the burst seams in the dress.

The hat was the crowning glory! It was huge and plastered with fresh flowers. Coloured ribbons streamed from the brim and the hat was firmly tied under Nan's plump chin in a big pink bow.

The whole village had turned out to see Eimear's arrival, for no one would miss Nan Sweeney's annual welcome of her granddaughter to Magherabeg. After the life had almost been hugged out of her and her case had been stored on the cart, Eimear settled herself beside her Nan and they set off home. The procession was headed by Nan's three identical border collies, Rory, Aonghas and Bran. They skipped ahead, white-tipped tails dancing high, clearing the way for their mistress and their important guest.

It isn't often that an ordinary girl from Derry gets to feel like a princess but Eimear could be sure of it one day in every year. The villagers waved and smiled and Nan dipped her head in dignified acknowledgement. Eimear blushed and giggled and called hello to the familiar faces. All in all, she had a whale of a time.

As they turned off the main road at the top of the village and headed towards the sea and the cottage, Oscar quickened his pace and Nan launched into a poem. She was prone to do this when she was emotional. This time it was one of her favourites and one familiar to Eimear. It was by William Butler Yeats, the greatest poet the world had ever seen—according to Nan.

The poem was "The Stolen Child" and it was beautiful. It told of the efforts of the fairies to lure a child away to a land of mystery and magic, and Eimear had an uncanny feeling that this was exactly what was happening to her. Bursting with happiness she too chanted the haunting verse,

Come away, O human child!
To the waters and the wild
With a faery, hand in hand,
For the world's more full of weeping
than you can understand.

2

An Unpleasant Surprise

Nan's cottage was snugly wrapped in hedges of fuchsia and wild honeysuckle. The air throbbed with the hum of insects and was heavy with scent. Nan had scraped out a garden from the weeds and rocks, and blossoms of every variety strained and stretched to show off. There were scented stocks and Canterbury bells, lupins and pansies and sweet William, wallflowers and roses of all sorts. Oh, there were hundreds of flowers that Eimear could see and smell but couldn't name. There was no order in the garden. Every available space had been planted, lavished with loving care and let grow in peace.

After feasting her eyes and nose, Eimear helped her Nan to unharness Oscar and then, unable to contain herself any longer, she set off at a gallop across the field, the three dogs leaping and twisting at her heels.

"I'm going over to see the Farrellys," she shouted back to her Nan. "I won't be long."

"Eimear, love..." Nan began but she was too late. Eimear had scrambled over a rock and disappeared from sight. Nan sighed. Eimear was in for a sore disappointment and Nan Sweeney did not hold with disappointment.

The roof of the cottage was just visible as Eimear reached half-way across the field and she could see a thin trail of smoke winding from the chimney. This sign that there was someone at home sent an electric current of excitement zizzing up her spine. She was going to see Kate again! Kate—her extra-special friend in paradise!

"Kate!" she shouted as she stood atop the last rock and gazed down at the unnaturally quiet cottage.

"Kate! Ronan! Josie! Brendan!...Anybody! It's me—Eimear!"

No mad tumble greeted her joyous shouts. The door remained tightly shut and not a curtain twitched.

Puzzled, Eimear slid off the rock and approached the door with a little more stealth. The dogs too had changed their tactics. They had split up and were sliding along, almost on their bellies, approaching the cottage from three different directions. Eimear could sense their suspicion. The door was shut tight. She almost knocked but then she felt silly. She had never knocked on this door in her life; it was always open to welcome her. She crept to the window and rested her nose on the sill, hoping to find out what was going on inside.

"Is this the way people behave around here?"

The booming voice jolted her and she almost cracked her teeth on the concrete windowsill.

Dazed, she swirled round and there stood a black giant

surrounded by the cowering, snarling dogs. The man towered well above Eimear and she had to tilt her head back to get a good look at him. He was dressed from neck to ankles in a black rubber suit and his whole head seemed to sprout black oily hair. He was carrying a cylinder of oxygen and loads of intricate-looking equipment.

"I...I...I was only looking for my friends the Farrellys," stammered Eimear, trembling in her runners. "They stay here every summer."

Somewhere between the wild shoulder-length hair and the great bushy black beard there had to be eyes, nose and mouth, but Eimear could barely see them.

"You'll not find them this summer," the deep voice growled from the tangled growth. "So get yourself on out of here and take these brutes with you."

He aimed a vicious kick at Aonghas, who had begun to sniff at his heel, but fortunately the dog was too quick for him and deftly dodged the blow. But the animals were as confused as Eimear. Never in all their lives had a cross word been spoken to them and they didn't know what to make of it at all.

"Tell Mrs Sweeney if she can't keep her pets and her pests out of my hair then I shall have to find other accommodation. I want privacy and I don't want nosy little brats like you messing about with my equipment."

He bent low over Eimear and a nose emerged from the hair and almost speared her. "Do you understand what I am saying?" he hissed. "*This place is out of bounds!*"

The trio of dogs, disturbed by the threatening tone of voice, regained some of their courage and began to growl again. This further enraged the hairy beast. Once again he swung at the dogs and once again he missed.

"Get out of here!" he roared. "And take those mangy fleabags with you. If I catch you around here again I won't be as reasonable as I was this time!"

Eimear ran and didn't stop until she was well out of sight of the cottage. Something was terribly wrong! Feeling worried and unhappy, she slowly made her way back to Nan Sweeney and safety. Nan was watching for her from her kitchen window. Poor Eimear! She was a picture of misery. If she'd had a tail it would have trailed forlornly along the ground like Rory's and Bran's and Aonghas's.

"You ran off before I could tell you, petal," soothed Nan as she wrapped Eimear in her arms. "The Farrellys didn't book the cottage this summer. I waited to the very last minute before renting it, hoping to hear from them, but there wasn't a word. Then two days ago this fellow turns up wanting to rent the cottage for at least three months. I think he works for a university or something—he has enough equipment for ten universities. I offered to do meals for him or at least send round some eggs and soda bread but he cut the nose off me. He doesn't want anybody near him. His work is very important, he says."

"He's horrible," sniffed Eimear. "How could you let him have the cottage, Nan? The Farrellys could turn up yet."

"I didn't like the look of him much myself," sighed Nan. "But beggars can't be choosers. I need to rent the cottage and the Farrellys would never turn up at this late stage, love."

"What's his name and what's he doing here, anyway?"

"Would you believe," smiled Nan, "he calls himself Diver, William Diver?" She was pleased to see a watery smile on Eimear's face. "But what he's doing here I haven't a notion. At first light he goes over the fields and down to the beach. I can hear the throb of the engine on his rubber dinghy as he heads out to sea and there's neither hilt nor hair of him until he chugs back in when it's almost dark."

Nan didn't like gloom so she gave Eimear a squeeze and said cheerfully, "You gave him a bit of a surprise today and perhaps, under all that hair, he's not the monster he seems to be. Sure maybe with time he'll soften up a wee bit and we'll invite him over for a bite of supper. Who knows? Perhaps you and the rubber gorilla will even become friends."

Maybe her Nan was right but Eimear had a feeling—a deep-down-in-the-pit-of-the-stomach feeling—that she and the Black Diver *were* destined to meet again and it would be an even more unpleasant meeting than their first.

🍎 🍎 🍎

3

Inishbwee

"We have to cheer ourselves up," Nan announced as she shook Eimear awake the next morning. "Come on, up you get. It's a glorious morning. We'll take a picnic and spend the day on Inishbwee."

No matter how rough the sea was, the water in the little cove that curled round the rocks below Nan's cottage was usually calm. It gently licked the soft white sand and, at full tide, it lapped against the steps that led up to the flower garden. Nan's sturdy boat was tied to an iron ring on the bottom step.

The boat was called *Báidín*, " little boat," and in Nan's opinion as good a name as any. Although it was a rowing-boat it also had a sail of sorts and a small outboard engine. Nan did not really approve of engines. "They are only for lazy people," she'd snort. "People who whizz past every-thing and see nothing."

But she was very conscious of how dangerous the sea

could be, so *Báidín* was equipped for every emergency. Life jackets were compulsory for all passengers and there was a good stock of flares and other odds and ends that Nan considered essential for survival at sea.

Today the tide had not quite reached the steps so they had to pull *Báidín* a few feet across the sand. Nan was wearing what she considered sensible clothes for outdoor pursuits. These consisted of a battered pair of corduroy trousers, wellies, a bright yellow jumper on which she had embroidered big yellow flowers with red centres, and a hat—but what a hat! It was of black felt with a huge floppy brim and a hole cut in the crown to let the fresh air in. Nan had pinned the brim up out of her eyes with an old nappy-pin and a bunch of artificial cherries. The brim was edged with white daisies that she had cut from an old tablecloth. The whole lot was tied beneath her chin with the tasselled cord of an ancient dressing-gown. Nan loved colours and she firmly believed in recycling worn-out goods.

The boat slid easily over the sand and soon it was floating on the clear water. Eimear climbed aboard and when she looked over the side she could see right down to the ripply sandy bottom. Small crabs scurried away from the disturbance and tiny, almost transparent fish darted hither and thither, faster than her eye could follow.

The three dogs plunged in after the boat, disturbing the calm water with their splashings and tail-waggings. Out and out they swam, never tiring, as Nan and Eimear pulled on the oars. They preferred to swim the short distance to the island on a warm day and Nan said it was good exercise for them. On and on they urged the boat until at last they landed on a tiny beach on Inishbwee.

Inishbwee means the "yellow island". Local people believe that it was given that name because most of the rocky surface is covered in whin bushes and there always seems to be at least one in bloom somewhere on the island, no matter the season. Nan Sweeney liked to gather the blossoms of the whin to make dye and she had something to dye almost every week. She was constantly gathering lichens and seaweeds, nettles and leaves, tree bark and wild flowers to produce the wonderful colours that brightened her curtains, cushions, tablecloths and bed covers. Living in Nan Sweeney's house was like living inside a rainbow.

Eimear always loved a trip to Inishbwee but this one was extra-special. They were going to spend the night there. Nan had brought bread, milk, tea and homemade jam with her. Everything else they needed they would find on the island.

"I'll show you how to survive on God's good gifts," Nan promised.

Once they reached shore Nan whisked Eimear and the dogs off on the "Grand Tour." This meant a lesson on the history of the island. It was a lesson Eimear had heard many times but she never tired of it.

"Ah, if we could but see the grandeur of those days," Nan sighed as they stood in the Carraig Rua, the ruins of an old castle that clung to a rocky promontory on the far side of the island. It had been built to keep a watch for raiding warriors from the north. Here the full force of the Atlantic beat against towering cliffs, and whirling seabirds screamed into the wind.

"The chieftain and his family would be seated here at the top of the table and beside them would be the favourite warrior and the harper and the poet and the storyteller."

Nan was pacing round the overgrown floor arranging her dinner party. "Ach but it's the great night's crack they would have had, feasting and dancing and listening to the tales of great deeds from the story teller. And MacSweeneys they all were. Don't you forget that, my girl. It's royal blood that's in your veins."

Eimear had heard this story often but it was always fresh to her. She listened, rapt, as the tale unfolded of how the chieftains were stripped of their lands and the people left to fend for themselves. The Sweeneys and the other island families had made the best of what the island had to offer.

"From earliest times there were MacSweeneys and McGinleys, O'Donnells and McFaddens living on this island, for hundreds of years right up until about fifty years ago, when they started leaving to look for the soft life. Nowadays people can't live without their televisions and washing machines and fancy cars. And the young ones think they're buried alive unless they have two-storey schools and disco dances."

While Nan was talking, Eimear was distracted by a movement in the sea to the north of the island beneath the craggy cliffs. It puzzled her for a while. She thought at first it was a seal bobbing up and down but then she saw a rubber dinghy. The bobbing head approached the dinghy and a sleek body hauled itself aboard. It was the Black Diver from Nan's cottage!

Eimear watched fascinated as her Nan rattled on. The man was absorbed for a time with something he had brought up from the water but then he stood up and threw a small object far out into the sea. Although she was a good distance away Eimear could sense his annoyance. He slid over the side of the dinghy again and, as smoothly as a cormorant diving for fish, disappeared under the green-tinged water.

At that moment a great cloud of seagulls rose wheeling and crying from the cliffs, and swooped out to the spot where the Black Diver had disappeared. They circled there in a great noisy whirlpool before settling back on the cliff face again.

"Noisy divils, aren't they?" Nan had noticed Eimear's preoccupation. "I believe the gulls on that particular cliff do more wailing than gulls anywhere else on earth. Some say that seagulls are the souls of people drowned at sea and that is why their cry is so sorrowful. But, then, folk talk an awful lot of nonsense, don't they?" The skin all over Eimear's body prickled and she felt as if every hair were standing on end. She looked again at the cliffs and the water but all was still and calm and very peaceful. Her father always said her imagination worked overtime. She pulled herself together and followed Nan, who was continuing the tour.

The walk through what remained of the village saddened Eimear. The ruins of the houses were still there, looking almost as they did on the day they had been abandoned fifty years before. The walls were sturdy but most of the thatched roofs had caved in and great clumps of nettles and thistles were growing out of them. But the outlines of the gardens were still visible, the village well still pumping crystal-clear water.

"We'll sleep in our old house," Nan announced. "It will need a bit of clearing up but it should be all right. There's a fair bit of roof left, enough to shelter us if it rains. We'll go food-collecting first and then we'll see about bedding. Look there," she directed Eimear. They had climbed down the rocks towards the beach and crossed to where a small stream met the sea. "Do you see what is clinging to those rocks?"

"Mussels," said Eimear. She knew what they were after: she had come collecting them before.

"There's food all around us, you know," Nan preached, "but the Irish are just plain rotten at seeing what is there for the taking."

Eimear waded into the warm, slightly muddy water and reached down below the surface to find the plumpest and juiciest shellfish.

"Take only what we can eat," instructed Nan. "Never over-harvest; then there will always be a good supply for man and creature."

Eimear loved the mussels now but when she first tasted one she had spat it out. She kept trying and gradually she grew to like them. They were so easy to cook too. They had only to be rinsed under running water, put in a large pot and placed over the fire. They cooked in their own juices and were ready when they opened up. They were delicious with a thickly buttered wadge of Nan's bread.

All this while Aonghas, Rory and Bran were busily chasing rabbits. It was a game they never won. The rabbits were far too quick for them. They seemed to sit in a trance until the dogs were almost upon them and then they scuttled towards their burrows, their white scuts cocked cheekily to mock the crestfallen collies.

"Mighty hunters, aren't they?" laughed Nan. "We'd starve to death if we were depending on them."

After the gathering of the food came the gathering of the bedding. In one part of the island the ferns grew to an alarming height. Eimear didn't like the dense jungle that swallowed her whole and towered above her head in gigantic fronds that blocked out the sunlight.

"There's nothing to be afraid of in here," Nan assured her. "Mind you, I don't mind a nice bit of fear now and then. It's the salt that flavours the imagination."

The ground from which the ferns sprouted was spongy and boggy and Eimear sank into the oozy slime until it was in danger of slithering over the tops of her wellies. Her boots made loud sucking noises as she struggled to move her feet. Soon she found that she couldn't move at all.

"Nan," she shouted. "Nan, I'm stuck!"

Her Nan had gone ahead and was busily slicing through the ferns with a sharp knife. Eimear was sure she couldn't be heard and she began to panic. All around her there were weird rustlings in the ferns and, more than anything else in the whole world, Eimear hated rats. She was a prisoner of the slime now, and if one of those disgusting beasts with the evil eyes and trailing, naked tail came out of the ferns and crawled around her feet she could not escape!

Suddenly the ferns began to tremble and the air grew cold—very cold. There was something there and Eimear knew it wasn't a rat. She felt as if some being was pulling her, luring her towards the very heart of the forest of ferns. She was overcome by a feeling of great loss and desperate sadness, crushed by a terrible longing that she did not understand.

Through the lacy patterns of the spreading foliage a shape began to form, a shimmering, hazy shape. Then suddenly the shape became solid and she could see a face. It was the face of a girl and she had the most startling blue eyes Eimear had ever seen. The yearning in those eyes was fierce. The girl beckoned Eimear forward and the eyes begged for help. Eimear wanted away from the ferns and the suffocating atmosphere that had closed in around her. But most of all she wanted away from those eyes!

"Nan! Nan!" she screamed hysterically.

She felt herself being lifted bodily from her wellies and carried to the edge of the jungle.

"There you are," said Nan laughing as she dumped her on a grassy bank. "Now what is all the howling about? Sure I thought Old Nick himself was after you!"

"There was something in there, Nan. Something weird."

"There's your divil," Nan laughed, as Rory emerged from the ferns and lolloped towards them.

Now that she was safe in the sunshine, Eimear wasn't really sure that she had seen anything at all. She knew that she didn't want to talk about it—even to Nan. So she laughed and looked foolish and wiped the muck from the boots that Nan had retrieved. She felt an arm round her shoulder and she buried her head in the flowers on Nan's jumper. Nan lifted Eimear's chin and gave her a searching look. She seemed troubled by something.

"You know, Eimear," she said, "there were always women on this island who could see things and hear the whisperings of souls who lived here long before them. I hope you're not going to be one of them."

"Nan, I don't know what you're talking about. What do you mean?"

Nan Sweeney could see that she had disturbed Eimear. She gathered up her bundle of ferns and laughed. "Sure I'm as bad as yourself at the imaginings. I'm only taking a rise out of you. I listened to too many fireside stories when I was your age. Come on now, I'm famished. It's time we had the dinner on."

In spite of her scary experience Eimear discovered that she was starving, and she hurried to help her Nan back to the house with the bedding. The meal was a magnificent feast. Nan had gathered potatoes and mint that grew wild in the old gardens and she cooked them over an open fire along with the mussels. A good dry box of matches was another essential that Nan always had stored on *Báidín*.

"It's all very well rubbing sticks or scraping stones," she said, " but sure a body would be dead of the hunger before a decent blaze got going." When Eimear had mopped up the delicious juices Nan produced a pot of her homemade blackberry jam which she knew was Eimear's favourite.

"It's the last pot," she said as she spooned dollops of it onto the bread. "The new crop won't be ready for a few weeks yet."

Eimear had a sudden memory of picking blackberries with the Farrellys and she felt sad that they wouldn't be here this year. She snuggled down under the ferns. It was cosy lying there close to Nan. She felt safe and happy. She fell asleep almost immediately and neither Black Divers nor whispering souls disturbed her dreams.

4

Ban Nolan

Next day, after they had filled Nan's baskets with whin blossoms, they set off for home. The weather was still beautiful, which is quite unusual for that part of the world, as it is known to rain and blow a fair bit in Donegal. The tide was in so they were able to row right up to the steps. They tied the boat up and heaved the baskets of blossoms up to the door of the cottage.

Eimear was so busy with her task that she didn't notice the darting, furtive movements behind the rocks in the field. She was just about to go inside when a terrible, raucous clamour split the quiet peace of the morning, causing her to leap with fright.

Saucepan lids were banged together, buckets were hammered with spoons and a deafening chorus of whooping Indian calls filled the air. A startled Oscar ceased his contented grazing, raised his head and bellowed a mighty hee-haw in protest. Not to be outdone, the dogs joined in with ear-splitting yowls.

Eimear dropped the blossoms and whirled round, her eyes popping in amazement when she saw the source of the noise. There, on four different rocks, stood four grinning Farrellys!

There was great confusion and excitement then as the Farrellys—mother, father and five children—piled into Nan's kitchen. Everybody was talking at once. Eimear was trying to tell Kate about her night on the island, Mrs Farrelly was trying to explain to Nan about why they hadn't booked the cottage, and the twins were just shouting to get attention. Finally Nan set the twins down on the doorstep with wedges of pie and tumblers of cordial and the others seated themselves round Nan's table to sip tea, admire the new baby and sort out stories.

Mr Farrelly's job had been the cause of the mix-up about the cottage. He was a teacher and that was why the family could spend the two months of summer in Donegal. He had applied for another job that hadn't the long holidays but he didn't get it. By the time he got the word it was already too late to book the cottage. Nobody seemed a bit put out about the job and that was probably because they had just bought themselves a good sturdy, second-hand caravan. They had written immediately to Nan telling her they were coming and asking permission to park the caravan in her field. The letter was there lying behind the door. It had arrived after Nan and Eimear had gone to Inishbwee. Nan was delighted to have the company and wouldn't hear tell of the family paying rent. Mr Farrelly said he wouldn't stay unless she accepted it. So she did and was grateful for it.

Kate and Eimear were ecstatic to be together again. Although both had friends at home, their summer friendship was special. Ronan Farrelly had often been the third member of their trio but this year Eimear hardly recognised him. He had grown so tall and seemed so grown-up. He sat apart from Kate and Eimear, looking bored with their chatter and fed up with the world in general.

"What's up with him?" whispered Eimear.

"Don't take him under your notice," sighed Kate. "He's just huffing. He didn't want to come. He's got a girl-friend," she giggled.

Eimear stared at Ronan; then she too began to giggle. She couldn't imagine him with a girl-friend. Ronan knew they were talking about him. He blushed a fierce red, threw Kate a poisonous look and stamped out the door, stepping in a piece of pie as he went. This set the twins howling and sent Ronan into a deeper rage. Kate and Eimear, the brats, laughed till their sides were sore.

Although Nan Sweeney tried to be self-sufficient, by growing all her own vegetables and living off the land, there were some things that had to be obtained elsewhere. As she had no cow, one of these was fresh milk. She could have bought it with the rest of her groceries in the village but instead she went every day to get her milk from Ban Nolan.

Ban Nolan was a tiny scrap of a woman who was very ancient and very odd. She lived in a dilapidated cottage a few fields away from Nan and liked to keep herself to herself. She had lived on in Inishbwee long after everyone else had left and her name was really a nickname. While she was on the island people had called her *Bean an Oileáin*, "woman of the island," and now it had become Ban Nolan. No one, except perhaps Nan Sweeney, was exactly sure what her real name was. It was Nan Sweeney's mother who had finally persuaded the old woman to leave the island and to settle in the old cottage.

Ban Nolan kept a few poultry and two skinny cows which she let wander free to graze on grassy verges or in any field that happened to have an open gate. Nan liked to keep an eye on the old woman but that was not easy as she was very independent. So they had set up a barter system. Every day Nan brought a bite of dinner and a scone when she baked and Ban Nolan filled her jug with milk.

"No, I am not coming with you," declared Nan as she pushed the jug into Eimear's unwilling hands. "Kate will go with you. You're just being silly. Ban Nolan won't take a bite out of you." Nan knew that Eimear was afraid of the old woman and thought it was about time she got to know her properly.

Eimear had never gone to Ban Nolan's cottage without Nan and she didn't want to go now. The old woman had odd ways and a strange look about her. She sometimes wandered the roads with her cows, muttering to herself or whistling to the blackbirds. Often she could be seen standing for hours on end, still as a statue, on a piece of high ground staring out across the sea towards Inishbwee.

"There are things to be afraid of in this world, Eimear, and things to value and respect," lectured Nan Sweeney in her soft, cajoling voice. "It is time you learned the difference. And remember, just because Ban Nolan dresses a bit different from everybody else doesn't mean there's something wrong with her."

Well, Eimear thought to herself, on the subject of peculiar dress sense Nan Sweeney should be an expert. But she kept her thoughts to herself.

Eimear was not happy as she lifted the basket of scones and a jug of thick vegetable soup and trudged across the field to meet Kate.

"She gives me the creeps," she confided in her friend as they made their way towards Ban Nolan's cottage. Kate had no creeps—far from it! She had seen the old woman often and heard all the stories about her weird habits but she had never spoken to her nor been to her cottage. She was just dying to see inside.

"I hope she asks us in," she jabbered. "Everybody says she has geese and hens and all sorts and they just wander in and out of the house...and there's cats...millions of them..." She rattled on excitedly but Eimear wasn't listening to her: she was lost in her own thoughts.

The door of the cottage was open slightly but there was no sign of life except for the cats who curled themselves around the girls' bare legs purring madly or opened one eye to observe them from their sun-drenched window-sills. They were sleek, contented felines of every breed and colour. Their glossy coats and air of self-satisfaction were the result of an easy life feeding on the cream from the speckled cows.

Eimear tapped on the door with two fingertips. It wasn't much of a door. It was hanging drunkenly away from the top hinge and the wood was worn and bleached by the sun.

"Ban…uh…Mrs…"

Eimear realised she didn't know what to call the old woman. She cleared her throat and began again timidly, "Am…ah…hello…it's me…Eimear…Eimear Kelly. I've come for the milk."

There was no answer.

"She's not in," she said with relief. "I'll leave the basket and Nan can come back later for the milk. Come on; let's get out of here."

But Kate would have none of that. She had come this far; she was going inside.

"I'm not leaving till I see the witch's den," she said, heaving the door until it scraped a few inches more across the floor and left a gap wide enough for her to squeeze through. "We'll have plenty of time. She's probably out talking to the trees or something."

Before Eimear could stop her Kate was inside the cottage. Eimear wanted to drop the basket and run but she couldn't abandon her friend. Besides, in a peculiar way, she wanted to see for herself where Ban Nolan lived.

"Where are you?" she whispered when she stepped across the threshold. It was very dark inside the cottage. The only light came from the half-open door and a very dirty window. After the brightness of the sunshine it was very difficult to see.

"Would you look at this!" Kate cried in delight. She had found a cardboard box full of kittens and had gone all gooey over them. Eimear's eye was taken with the heaps of books that were piled around the floor, on the window-sill and on the one and only chair. She had never associated Ban

Nolan with books. The chair, although worn and faded, was an elegant, padded velvet affair and out of keeping with the rest of the cottage. She moved around the books, afraid to touch them, and almost bumped into a small table in a corner. It was scattered with pages, very old crackly pages— covered with tiny, neat handwriting.

"What have you found?"

Kate was peering over her shoulder.

"What's written on them?"

Kate reached out to grab the pages and instinctively Eimear clutched at her hand.

"Don't touch them!" she whispered.

"What's up with you?" Kate demanded, highly offended. "Sure they're only a bunch of old papers."

"We shouldn't touch them," replied Eimear. "They're none of our business."

Kate shrugged her shoulders and went back to the kittens. She was an easygoing sort of a person and she wasn't really interested in the old pages anyway. Eimear stood looking at the papers. The light was too dim to read any of the tiny script but just seeing it there caused her heart to race and made her feel very uneasy. She was about to turn away from the table when a sudden shaft of sunlight shone directly through the open door and lit up the dark corner.

An oval-framed picture on the wall was spotlighted by the dust-speckled beam. It was an old photograph and from the brown tinted background, a young girl smiled. A halo of burnished curls framed a pair of clear, light eyes set in a small pale face. The eyes disturbed Eimear. The girl wore a high-necked, frilly blouse; around her delicate neck hung a chain and on the chain hung a cross. It was a magnificent cross. It was decorated with swirling leafy patterns and had five coloured stones—one on each arm of the cross and a dark one in the middle. Eimear reached out to trace the swirls with her finger.

Suddenly the corner went dark and a soft voice spoke from the doorway,

"It's very beautiful, isn't it?" The voice was neither friendly nor threatening. It was clear and musical. Guiltily Eimear withdrew her hand. It was very embarrassing to be found poking about someone's house. She braced herself and turned to face Ban Nolan. She found herself staring into a pair of light-blue eyes.

"You let yourselves in then?" said Ban Nolan amiably. "That's grand. I wasn't expecting company today."

The two girls stood still, struck dumb for a few seconds, until Eimear managed to stammer, "I'm s-s-sorry, Miss...ah...Ban...ah. We didn't mean any harm."

"Well then, I'm sure there's no harm done," smiled the old woman, coming further into the room. She was accompanied by two huge ganders who stretched their necks and hissed menacingly at the intruders. Kate gave a sharp, frightened yelp and crouched in against the wall.

"Stop showing off!" Ban Nolan scolded the ganders. "Away out with the pair of you."

The ganders pulled in their necks obediently and, waggling their plump behinds, padded out on their big orange feet.

Ban Nolan was a rare sight. She wore three skirts of three different lengths, a pair of rubber boots turned down at the top and with a hole in one toe, an assortment of cardigans and a man's battered hat pulled well down over her head. In her hand was a stick—not a fancy stick, just something she found along the road. She was never seen without a stick and used it to poke in the hedges for hens' nests or to guide her cows home for milking.

"I've come for the milk," said Eimear. "My Nan...Mrs Sweeney sent me."

"Come over here, child, till I get a good look at you."

Ban Nolan had cleared the chair of books and had seated herself with her back to the window.

Reluctantly, Eimear moved out of the shadows and approached the old woman. Two gnarled and knotted hands reached out and held her arms tightly but not painfully. The clear blue eyes seemed to bore right through Eimear so that she felt they knew even her very own secret dreams and fears.

"What is your name, child?" asked Ban Nolan.

"Eimear, Miss...Eimear Kelly," answered a nervous Eimear.

"Eimear. It's a good name—a strong name. Eimear, the bride of the Hound of Ulster, the strongest warrior in Ireland. Do you know that story?"

"Yes," said Eimear. "My Nan tells it to me."

"Yes, you're Sorcha Sweeney's grandchild. You come from good people, Eimear Kelly. The MacSweeneys were a courageous tribe and had a great love of poetry. They knew about the world beyond our own everyday one."

Eimear felt she was being weighed up, her worthiness judged—but for what?

"I hope you have the Sweeney courage, Eimear Kelly," said Ban Nolan and then added, almost under her breath, "I think you might need it."

Looking into those strange eyes, Eimear felt again the pull of the mysterious force that she had met on the island of Inishbwee. She knew also that Ban Nolan felt it too.

"Evil and greed are with us again, Eimear Kelly, and I am too old for the battle. It is time for another to take over."

At these words a flush of fear swept over Eimear. The gnarled hands tightened their grip on her arms. She felt strength flowing through them and into the marrow of her bones.

"Your Nan should be proud of you," smiled Ban Nolan. She dropped her hands and rose painfully from the chair.

"Come now and get your milk. Thank your Nan for her kindness. You must come and see me again."

As they warily passed the gander guards the old woman called after them, "Birds are creatures of great wonder, you know. They can fly through the air and under the waters and between worlds. But beware the Black Diver. He is not seeking fish."

"What was she blathering on about?" Kate asked. She was skipping over the grass, glad to be back out in the sunshine.

"I think she's got a few loose wires. Mind you, she *is* creepy. I'm not going back there." Then she burst out laughing. "Evil and greed are with us again, Eimear Kelly," she chanted in an over-the-top imitation of Ban Nolan's voice. "Definitely a looney bin." The laughter rippled from her throat and up into the clear air.

"Come on quick back to the caravan till we tell Ronan. Maybe it'll bring a smile to his miserable face."

"No," said Eimear quietly. "You go on. I have to take the milk back to Nan."

Kate looked at her thoughtfully. "You didn't believe her, did you? You're not letting that daft old eejit give you the heebie-jeebies, are you?"

"Don't talk daft yourself," said Eimear. "I'll call for you after tea."

Before going into the cottage Eimear stood and looked out towards Inishbwee. It looked very peaceful. A coal-black cormorant popped up from the water and shook its long neck before diving again. It was doing what all cormorants do: it was looking for fish. Eimear gave herself a shake. She was thinking of the other much larger Black Diver she had seen on the far side of Inishbwee, and Ban Nolan's words rang through her head.

"Beware the Black Diver. He is not seeking fish."

🥀 🥀 🥀

5

Strange Goings-On

For the next couple of weeks, Eimear tried to put all thoughts of strange other worlds and battles against greed and evil firmly out of her mind. The weather continued beautiful and so the children spent all the daylight hours on the beach or paddling around in *Báidín*. They swam and fished in rock pools, ate mountains of gritty sandwiches and built acres of sand castles. There was a lovely sense of tranquillity about the long summer days.

Eimear had not gone again for the milk to Ban Nolan's cottage and she had almost forgotten the old woman's words. Then one day she was sitting in the field making a daisy-chain. All of a sudden she knew that someone was watching her. She looked around and saw, in a gap in the hedge, clear blue eyes peering from under a battered hat. The eyes were disturbed. They seemed to be sending a message to Eimear—a warning or an appeal for help, she wasn't sure which. Then they were gone, swallowed up by the hedge.

This incident upset Eimear. She felt she should be doing something, but didn't know what it was she was supposed to do. She saw threats in everything. When she was bringing in the clothes from the line one day, a huge black crow settled on the pole that supported the line and sat there perfectly still, staring at her with its yellow eyes.

"Shoo, you great ugly bag of feathers!" she shouted, throwing a T-shirt at it. The bird took off with such squawking and flapping that Eimear had to laugh. She had terrified the poor thing and it was only trying to steal some of the scraps that Nan had left out for the chickens. She decided then that it was time to put all silly notions out of her mind and get on with enjoying the holidays.

Ronan Farrelly had changed a lot since last summer. His voice was peculiar for a start; sometimes it was as smooth as ice-cream and at other times it was harsh and hoarse and as deep as doubt. He was mooning about the place, sighing and moping, and Nan said he had a face on him like a plateful of mortal sins. Eimear didn't know what that meant but it made her laugh anyway. She missed the old Ronan who had ducked her in the waves, kicked over her sand castles and led herself and Kate into all sorts of scrapes. This year, when he moved himself at all, Ronan usually didn't want company. He went off on his lief lone, weighed down with binoculars, a notebook and an assortment of jars.

"He's a scientist at the moment," explained Kate when they had all settled down for a lazy day on the beach. "You see, the girl-friend—her daddy is Ronan's biology teacher. He wanted to impress her so he entered the Young Scientist of the Year competition and now he's stuck with it. He has to come up with something brill or he thinks she'll dump him."

Eimear looked over towards Ronan. It was the first time he had come to the beach with them. The twins were digging holes and falling into them and she and Kate were stretched out like fat seals lapping up the sunshine. But Ronan was busy. He was settling himself in a niche in the rocks, complete with jars, notebook and binoculars.

"It's bogs he's studying, ye know," volunteered Kate. "Bogs! Brown water and turf! That takes a lot of looking into." She exploded into helpless giggles.

Again Eimear looked at Ronan. She felt a bit sorry for him. He didn't seem comfortable with life—it was hurting him like a shoe that didn't fit yet. She was glad that he had come to the beach.

"What are you at today?" Kate shouted, barely smothering her laughter. "There's no bogs in the Atlantic."

Ronan tried to ignore his little sister's taunting inquiry but he just couldn't let her get away with it. "You!" he spat between tight lips, "you think you know everything, don't you? Well, smart arse, I'm not looking at the sea; I'm looking at Inishbwee."

Now Kate was definitely not going to give her brother the satisfaction of asking why he was looking at Inishbwee. So she gave a bored yawn, turned over on her tummy and went to sleep.

Eimear, however, was curious. "What are you looking at on Inishbwee?" she asked, plonking herself down beside Ronan on his vantage point in the rocks.

"Nothing much," he answered begrudgingly. "There's a great big gorilla keeps getting in the way."

"In the way of what?" asked Eimear. Ronan sighed a deep sigh. He was going to have to explain to this child the importance of Irish bogs.

"Ireland is the last European repository of lowland bog," he instructed as he tried to see the words on the page of his geography book. "Elsewhere, the bogs have been drained and the natural habitat, a remnant of the Ice Age, is disappearing along with the wildlife and the plants that support it." He was quite pleased with his performance and he added as an after-thought, "Inishbwee has some lovely untouched bogland and I'm thinking of going over there to do an intensive study."

Ronan was pleased with himself but Eimear's eyes had glazed over with boredom and she was about to slide back down to the warm sand to join Kate when she remembered something Ronan had said.

"What do you mean, some gorilla keeps getting in your way?" she asked.

"A man," answered Ronan. "He seems to be digging chunks out of the bog. I hope he's not destroying anything."

"Let me see," she demanded, grabbing the binoculars from Ronan.

"Hey, have a bit of respect," scolded Ronan, as he unlooped the strap from his neck and made more room for her in his nest.

"I can't see a thing," complained Eimear. Ronan took the glasses from her and turned them round. "Try them this way," he said.

Eimear ignored his sarcastic tone of voice and put the correct end of the binoculars to her eyes. She swung them round in all directions, obeying Ronan's instructions, but still she could see only sky and ocean. Then suddenly everything came into focus and a black shape filled her vision. It was bending and straightening furiously. All around the furrowing creature were piles of soil. She swung the glasses again and saw the rubber dinghy bobbing in the water beside the little beach where they always landed in *Báidín*. The Black Diver had not only abandoned the waters off the far side of the island but had come ashore and was now working on the land!

Eimear remembered Ban Nolan's warning look from the gap in the hedge. Was this what she meant? Was the Black Diver doing something that alarmed the old woman? And if he was, what was she, Eimear Kelly from Derry, supposed to do about it? "Kate," she shouted, shoving the binoculars back into Ronan's hands, "pull on a T-shirt and come on!

"You're just a spoilsport," complained Eimear. "What's the matter with you anyway?"

Kate was nursing a bare foot and her humour wasn't the best. "You come at me with no warning and you drag me up here before I can even pull on my flip-flops. I stood on a thistle; and, anyway, I'm not going into that house," she said with a pout.

Eimear felt that Kate was just being awkward and she began to lose patience with her. "Why not?" she queried. "You weren't a bit slow to trespass in Ban Nolan's cottage.

What's the difference?"

"I wasn't afraid of Ban Nolan, but that hateful man, now: he's a different story.

"The Black Diver?"

"That's a good name for him," smiled Kate, beginning to come round a bit. "He found the twins playing about here and he chased them and then called at the caravan and told Mammy that if any of his equipment was damaged he'd have the gardaí on us. The twins are so terrified of him that they won't even come over to this side of the field."

"But he's over on Inishbwee now," urged Eimear. "He won't catch us."

"I shouldn't even be here," answered Kate. "Mammy warned me to stay away. I'm certainly not going inside."

"I don't want you to go in," Eimear continued coaxing. "I only want to look through the window. Sure there's no harm in that."

Eventually Kate was persuaded and the two girls approached the cottage with great care, even though they knew the occupant was well out of the way. They elbowed their way through the dry grass until they reached a cobbled area in front of the house and then crept on all fours until they were under the window-sill. There was really no need for all this caution but they enjoyed being stealthy.

The inside of the cottage was a great disappointment to Eimear. There wasn't a lot to be seen from the window but what she did see was very ordinary. The big living-room was neat and orderly and the doors leading into the other three rooms were tightly closed. "I know how to open these windows," Eimear whispered.

"Don't you dare!" Kate squeaked. "You said you weren't going in."

"I said I didn't want you to go in. I didn't say anything about me. I want to have a look inside."

"Why?" demanded Kate.

"I don't know," said Eimear, shrugging her shoulders. "There's something peculiar about the Black Diver and I want to find out what it is."

At this Kate collapsed into a heap of giggles. "I bet it's something to do with the rubbish Ban Nolan told you. You think there's something important about you, don't you? Some mystery that only you can solve!" And Kate laughed so hard the tears came streaming down her face.

Eimear was stung and hurt by Kate's mockery. "Go on home," she said coldly. "Go and play buckets and spades with the twins on the beach. I don't need you!"

This time it was Kate's turn to be offended. "OK, be like that," she huffed. "See if I care." And she flounced off in a temper.

Without casting a look after Kate, Eimear eased her fingers under the frame of the small window and jiggled and shoved until she freed the catch and it slid up, leaving a narrow opening. It was a tight squeeze and she ripped her T-shirt and scraped her knee in the effort but she managed to get through. Once inside, all the bravado left her and she felt lonely and afraid. She was sorry for being nasty to Kate and wished that her friend was still with her. She wanted to run away but she made herself stay. She wasn't leaving the cottage until she found out something about the Black Diver and tried to figure out how he, Ban Nolan, Inishbwee and Eimear herself were all tied up together.

She took a deep breath and then she began to open cupboards in the living-room, looking for anything extraordinary. She found crockery and cutlery, tins of beans and packets of corn flakes, washing-up liquid and oil-cans, but nothing that even the most lively imagination could find intriguing. She pushed open the door into the largest bedroom and found a neatly made bed and drawers full of socks, jumpers and underwear. The smallest bedroom was used as a store room for diving equipment, cameras, tools and boots and the middle room seemed to be used as a study. The bed in the middle-sized room was piled high with books and on the small table by the window was a very smart computer. There was nothing odd about this. If, as the man claimed, he was working with a university, then he would have plenty of books and a computer. Eimear didn't know what she expected to find but there was nothing here to rouse suspicion.

A huge chart covered one complete wall and Eimear climbed on the bed to get a good look at it. It had lines on it like the weather map on the television but nothing about wind or rain or temperatures. She looked more closely and saw that the lines were marked in fathoms. It was a map of the ocean with a large block of land in the middle. With a jolt of excitement, Eimear realised she was looking at a map of Inishbwee and the surrounding waters. On the far side of the island, offshore from the ruins of Carraig Rua, a forest of crosses were marked in pencil and beside each cross was written the word "Negative."

This chart told Eimear that the Black Diver was looking

for something in the sea near the cliffs of Carraig Rua, but she had guessed that already. It also told her that, whatever it was he was looking for, he had not found it. What it didn't tell her was *what* he was looking for and why he was now digging on Inishbwee.

As she was climbing off the bed she kicked one of the books and it tumbled onto the floor. It was a big, heavy, ancient book with tiny writing. She heaved it back onto the bed and noticed that there were some pictures in it, each covered with filmy tissue paper. She lifted the paper from the first picture and saw that it was just an old ship, one of those with loads of sails and rows of cannon sticking out of its bulging belly.

Eimear didn't find anything particularly interesting in the ship so she turned the next few pages. These were covered with coloured drawings of old-fashioned shoes, cups made out of horns and fancy hair-combs. The last page was full of jewellery. There were long gold chains, jewelled boxes, brooches and rings and fancy daggers. At the bottom of the page was a drawing of a cross. Eimear looked at it closely and then caught her breath. She couldn't be sure but it looked exactly like the cross she had seen around the neck of the young girl in the picture in Ban Nolan's house. Quickly she flicked through the pages trying to find out more about the cross, but the book was written in a strange language and she could not understand one word of it. She pushed the book aside in disgust and it slid towards the wall. As she reached to retrieve it she saw something jammed in the tiny gap between the bed and the wall. She pulled it out but it was only a cardboard folder. Why, she asked herself, would such an ordinary item be hidden away so carefully?

Eimear opened the folder and she found the answer. There were papers in the folder: old crackly papers covered in tiny handwriting—the papers she had seen in Ban Nolan's cottage. The Black Diver must have stolen them!

A faint squeak of a floorboard set Eimear's heart beating wildly. She held her breath and listened. The sound came again. There was someone in the living-room. The Black Diver had returned! The blood rushed to her head and she was gripped in a choking panic. She was trapped in the bedroom with no possibility of escape!

6

The Story Unfolds

Eimear crept quietly over to the door and listened again. She could hear nothing. Was her imagination playing tricks on her again? Whether it was or not, she desperately wanted to get out of that room and out of that cottage. Gently she opened the door and let it swing back. There was no sign of anybody in the room.

The open window was visible from the doorway and she decided she would make a run for it. She stepped over the threshold and stopped for a second to summon up her courage before making her dash to freedom. She was just about to take flight when a hand grabbed her T-shirt, pulling her back.

The panic drove her wild! She pulled and screamed, kicked out wildly behind her, and when she felt the hand relax its grip a little she tore away, doing more damage to the battle-torn T-shirt, and scrambled through the window.

She was half way over the field when she heard an

angry shout behind her. "You almost knocked my teeth out, you great, big, stupid elephant!"

Hanging out the cottage window was a very irate Kate!

"What were you doing there? I thought you had abandoned me!"

The two girls rolled round the grass laughing in the way you only can laugh when you have just frightened the daylights out of yourself.

"I came back," panted Kate. "I was afraid I'd miss something. Did you find anything?"

It was now that Eimear realised she was still clutching the blue folder.

"Yes," she said. "This."

"What is it?"

"It's the papers that were in Ban Nolan's house."

"Is that all? I thought it was something important."

"It *is* important," said Eimear hotly. "He must have sneaked into her house and stolen them."

"How do you know that?" asked Kate in reasonable tones. "Ban Nolan might have given them to him or maybe he borrowed them for a while. Just because he has them doesn't mean he stole them. You're the one who's done the stealing."

"Well, I think he did," argued Eimear. "If he'd just borrowed them why did he go to so much bother to hide them? There is something in these papers that he wants to know and I intend to find out what it is."

"How?" asked Kate.

"Read them of course, spud-head."

The two girls quite often exchanged insults like this, as

friends do, and only rarely did one or other take offence.

"Get Ronan's magnifying glass and come round to the cottage after supper. We'll read them together."

"But there's pages and pages of them!" protested Kate, who didn't believe in doing too much paperwork during the summer holidays. "I've a better idea," she said. "I'll lend you the magnifying glass and you can read them and then tell me what they are all about. I can't come round tonight, anyway. Mammy and Daddy are going out for a while. Ronan's in charge and I have to stay in."

Secretly Eimear was pleased that Kate didn't want to read the papers with her. She wanted to go through them inch by inch by herself and didn't know how she was going to explain this to Kate. Now she was saved the bother.

As soon as supper was over she told her Nan that she was going to bed early as she had something good to read. Her Nan was crocheting and listening to a play on the radio while keeping an ear open for any crisis in the Farrelly caravan, and didn't mind.

The long daylight hours of the summer allowed Eimear to read the papers without using Ronan's glass or putting on the light. She took them over to her favourite perch on her broad window-sill which looked out over the sea towards Inishbwee. It took her a while to be at ease with the old-fashioned writing but soon she was so deep into the story that she didn't notice the quaint language. It suited the tale that was unfolding before her eyes.

It was a story of such terror and sadness that Eimear could not put it down until she had turned the last stiff page.

In the spring of 1588 the inhabitants of Inishbwee planted their oats and tended their cattle, pigs and sheep. They spun their wool and wove the large blankets that served for cloaks and bedding and for keeping the draughts out of their small thatched cabins. What was happening in the world beyond Inishbwee rarely made any great difference to the lives of the islanders.

But now things were changing. There was great trouble throughout Ireland and the island's chieftain, Owen MacSweeney, was absent from his castle on the Carraig Rua. He had gone to help the more powerful chiefs in their battle with the forces of Queen Elizabeth. It was to be a long and bitter struggle for the survival of the rule of the Irish chieftains, the way of life of the people and ownership of the clan lands.

Owen's stories, when he returned to the island, disturbed his people. He told of the savagery carried out, not only against the Irish warriors but against the ordinary people ploughing their fields or hiding in their cabins. The islanders shivered with fear and blessed the sea which so far had saved them from such horrors.

Some of the chieftains had bowed to the power of the English throne in order to keep for themselves the land and the wealth of their territory. Others held out strongly and were prepared to fight to the death. Among these was Owen MacSweeney. He was often away for long periods, returning to his home only when he was exhausted and in need of a safe hiding-place.

It was in a state near death from tiredness and sadness that he returned to the island that spring. He had spent a bitter winter travelling the land, talking to the other chieftains and hiding from the soldiers who would have been delighted to capture and torture him and, when he would eventually have been allowed to die, display his head on a pole at a crossroads. He brought tales of people starving and living like animals in the woods after their homes had been burned to the ground and many of their kinsfolk slaughtered. There was none of the usual rejoicing on the island to welcome back their lord — no feasting in the castle, no playing of the harps, no dancing or singing of songs. Instead the people huddled together, whispering, and praying that the great evil would never reach their island.

They listened in tears as Owen told them of the sights he had seen and shook their heads sadly when they heard about a dream that had been lost. A large fleet of Spanish ships had sailed to England to invade that country and the Irish chieftains had hoped that a Spanish victory would be the saving of the Irish. The invasion had failed and now the Spanish ships were scattered in the storm-torn waters of the north Atlantic and could do nothing else but try to return to their homeland.

The people prayed for the poor souls on the ships and then went about their work wondering when their day of suffering would come.

All that month fierce storms raged around the island. The force of the huge waves carried the sea-water right up over the cliffs to batter against the foundations of Carraig Rua itself. The fishermen could not put their little skinboats to sea and so there was no fresh fish to eat, but there was a good supply of salted fish and enough oatmeal for porridge and oatcakes.

One night when the storm was at its height, a cry went up on the wind and was carried to every cabin. A ship, the like of which had never been seen before by the islanders, was floundering in the churning ocean and was in danger of being smashed on the jagged rocks below Carraig Rua.

Led by Owen MacSweeney, the people flocked to the clifftop, holding their rush lanterns against the storm, but there was little they could do. Helplessly they watched as the fat-bodied hulk with its broken masts and torn sails was swept onto the treacherous rocks and split in two as easily as snapping firewood. As the ship was swallowed by the hungry waters tiny figures could be seen clinging frantically to ropes and splinters of wood. A wail of grief went up from the huddled watchers as the tragedy was acted out before their eyes.

For two more days the storm raged and then on the third morning the ocean was miraculously calm, with barely a ripple disturbing its glassy surface. Owen MacSweeney ordered a search of the beaches and warned that any survivors should be shown the warm hospitality that was a tradition of their clan. Every rock cleft and sandy beach was scoured but not a sign of a soul, living or dead, was found.

Very little indeed was washed ashore from the ship. It had gone to the bottom taking all on board with it and was giving nothing up. Only fragments of wood littered the beach and the people gathered the stout oak to strengthen their cabins and byres.

Young Máire MacGinley had collected much of the

wood for her family and had left it in small piles so that her brothers could carry it back to the cabin. She was on the far side of the island, well away from her home, enjoying the bit of warm sun and thinking of the great drama she had seen the night of the shipwreck. She had seen boats sink before. Almost two years ago, when she was eight, she had stood on the same spot watching her father desperately trying to reach the island in his flimsy boat. For days her mother and the children had searched the beaches but Hugh MacGinley had never been seen again.

She shook herself out of her daydream and was just about to run up the grassy slope and get home before she got a scolding for not being there to milk the cow when she saw a bundle lying in the the long coarse grass that grew around the beach. She approached carefully, knowing full well what it was, but afraid to see what a drowned man looked like.

He looked as if he were just lying there sleeping. His dark hair curled around his pale face and his drooping moustache flowed over the long slim hand that supported his head. Sadly Máire turned away to go to find someone to carry the body back for burial, and then she heard a moan. The man was still alive!

She bent down towards him and touched him gently on the shoulder. "Can you hear me?" she whispered. "Are you in pain?"

The man opened his eyes and spoke to her in a weak voice but the words were in a language that Máire did not understand. The sad eyes asked the question, "Am I among friends or enemies?"

It was clear from the way the stranger was dressed that he was a man of some importance. His jacket was of red velvet and his shirt, although torn and dirty, was of the finest linen. A gold chain with large links was wound several times round his waist, and just peeping from a pouch slung on a leather belt was the jewelled shaft of a dagger. He had a single large ring on each hand and around his neck was a chain and cross. The cross was the most beautiful thing Máire had ever seen. It too was made of gold and worked in delicate designs of twining leaves. A bright red stone shone from the centre and four blue stones nestled at the end of each arm.

When Máire brought the news back to the islanders, Owen MacSweeney ordered that the man be carried to his castle and given every care and attention. His wet clothes were stripped from him and washed and his chains and leather pouch of jewelled ornaments put away carefully. The man was very ill. He was wandering in his mind, crying out in terror and despair.

Máire was given the task of looking after the stranger. This was a great honour but, in the eyes of the islanders, it was her right. Not only had she found him but her mother, Caitlín MacSweeney, was sister to the chieftain and so MacSweeney blood ran thick in Máire MacGinley's veins. The young girl searched the hillsides looking for wild herbs to make into medicines and fed him thin soups and sweet drinks made from the best honey. However, she was not to be left in peace to care for the gift from the ocean.

"The soldiers are coming!"

The cry went up at first light the morning after Máire's

discovery. The sinking of the Spanish galleon had been seen from the mainland and the soldiers were coming to search for survivors. Quickly Owen MacSweeney wrapped the Spaniard in blankets and took him to a dry cave usually used for storing butter, grain and salted meat. It was so well hidden that the soldiers would never find it. Máire was left to guard him and she was given enough food and fresh water to keep them both alive for several days. She was glad she had collected plenty of herbs. Owen himself and all the men took off to the wildest part of the island. If they stayed they would either be killed or captured. Because they knew the island so well they were certain they could move quickly from place to place and never be found. Máire's brothers, although only twelve and fifteen, went with the older men.

The women and children stood silently in a group beside the well around which their cabins were built. The soldiers questioned them about their menfolk and the whereabouts of Owen MacSweeney, and wanted to know if anyone had come ashore from the wrecked ship. The women didn't answer. Not only did they not want to give this information but they did not understand a word the soldiers were saying. Nobody on the island, except Owen MacSweeny, could speak any language other than their own Irish tongue.

The silence angered the soldiers and, in a frenzy of destruction, they tore the cabins apart. Then they roamed the island searching for anyone they could find, but the men were too clever for them and the cave was impossible to find. Carraig Rua was ransacked and anything of value stolen or broken.

The women prayed aloud that their homes would not be put to the torch and their prayers were answered. The wind got up again and the soldiers, fearful that they would be stranded on the island, took to their boats. They took with them as much food as they could carry and many of the bright woollen blankets to keep them warm on cold nights. They would have taken some of the pigs too but they were afraid of overloading their boats and being tossed into the now choppy seas. Instead they slaughtered as many as they could catch.

When the soldiers left, Owen and the men returned. They did their best to repair the cabins but they were very angry at what they saw. It was decided that it would be safer if the stranger remained in the cave at least for the summer months. In the winter they would build him a cabin near enough to the cave so that he could hide there when danger threatened.

Máire MacGinley was the stranger's constant companion. During that long warm summer she nursed him back to health. At first he didn't speak at all and when he did Máire could not understand what he was trying to say. Every morning she left her own home and came with food to the lonely cave. The man was usually sitting on the tiny pebble beach at the entrance to the cave gazing out across the Atlantic. The chieftain had restored the pouch of golden ornaments to the unexpected guest and usually he wore it strung round his waist.

Gradually they learned a little of each other's language. The Spaniard had been the captain of the ill-fated ship and his name was Don Antonio Serralles. He had a wife and family back in Spain, in a place he called Valencia, and a daughter almost the same age as Máire. He was very sad and very lonely. He longed to return to his home.

Owen MacSweeney hoped that it might be possible to smuggle Don Antonio off the island and sneak him aboard a friendly ship bound for a European port. The Spanish captain waited eagerly for news every time Owen went on one of his trips to the mainland. But the situation there was getting worse. The soldiers were everywhere and a sharp watch for Spanish survivors was being kept at the ports.

The years passed and Don Antonio lost hope of ever seeing his home and family again. Máire was heartbroken for him. She had grown fond of him. He was a very gentle man like her father and she sometimes wondered if the ocean had given Don Antonio into her care in place of the father it had stolen from her. The islanders kept a respectful distance from Don Antonio. They were shy of strangers anyway and there was the problem of not understanding what he was saying.

So he relied entirely on Máire for company, and just as she began to look on him as a father, he began to care for her as the daughter he would never see again. He told her stories of his home and Máire listened rapt, not understanding all the words but following the meaning of the tale. They developed a language of their own, half Spanish and half Irish.

Time and again Don Antonio told Máire of his longing to see his home in Valencia but as the years passed he knew that that would never be.

"I will never be buried in the warm soil of my own

country," he said one day when he had been about five years on the island and Máire was now a young woman of fifteen. "So promise me that when I die you will give my body to the cold ocean so that I may rest in the green depths with my shipmates and fellow-countrymen." Máire did not want to talk about death so she would turn the conversation in another direction or pretend she didn't understand what he was talking about. Don Antonio would not give up and one day his plea was so earnest that she knew he would rest more contented if she made the promise. So, very solemnly, Máire promised that when Don Antonio Serralles died he would be be buried at sea, at the exact spot where his ship had foundered. To Máire it was a binding promise. In those times, the people of Inishbwee believed that a solemn vow had to be kept, even under threat of death.

Don Antonio did seem to become more cheerful when he knew that one day he would rejoin his crew, and at times when the sun was warm he even seemed happy. Máire didn't worry about her promise. Don Antonio was still quite young and would live for many years.

Not everyone on the island, however, was concerned about the well-being of Don Antonio Serralles. There was one who was interested only in the Spaniard's wealth. Conor MacFadden was a very discontented young man. The hard life on the island did not please him at all, and he longed to leave and seek an easier existence

Máire had grown into a very beautiful young woman and secretly Conor hoped to marry her. He was sure that the Spaniard would give Máire his gold and jewels one day and then they could leave the island with their treasures and have a good life on the mainland.

To his great anger, when she was seventeen, Máire married a young man who was a particular favourite of Owen MacSweeney and who always accompanied the chief on his visits to the mainland. Conor watched the young couple build a home for themselves and the jealousy grew in him like a poisonous boil. He was determined to get both his revenge and the Spaniard's wealth.

Conor began to plot and plan. He would kill the Spaniard and steal his gold; then he would betray Owen MacSweeney and his faithful companions. He had listened greedily to his chieftain's tales of the burning of castles and the confiscation of lands. If he offered information about the plans of the rebellious chiefs, then surely the English would reward him with gold and some good land far away from the wilderness of Inishbwee? Like all cowards, Conor MacFadden could plot but he hadn't the courage to carry out his evil intentions. So he watched and waited and grew more bitter and envious until something happened that inflamed his greed. Máire had a beautiful baby daughter and named her María after the stranger's daughter. The Spaniard was godfather to the child and at the ceremony he presented the tiny baby with his beautiful jewelled golden cross. Conor could see that all the Spaniard's wealth would go in gifts to Máire's children and so would end up in the hands of the husband. His hatred and jealousy now knew no bounds.

The war on the mainland had grown worse. The chieftains were now fighting to the death. Owen MacSweeney gathered all the young men of the island and asked them to go with him to join the great Ulster earls, Hugh O'Neill and Hugh O'Donnell, in their courageous stand against their powerful enemy. Máire's husband and brothers eagerly stood by their chieftain's side. So did all the young men, including Conor MacFadden.

On the morning their menfolk left the island the women gathered to wish them luck and bid them a tearful farewell. As he was climbing over some rocks to get to the boats, Conor MacFadden slipped and injured his leg. He made a heroic effort to walk but he thought the limb was broken. His disappointment at not being able to sail with the departing warriors was quite touching to see.

The young men consoled him and asked him to see to the women and children while they were away. Máire's husband especially asked him to take care of his young wife and daughter. Conor promised and nobody noticed the evil little smile on his lips as the boat pulled away.

There was great sadness on the island after the men left. Máire's mother left her own cabin and moved in with Máire, for the company and to help look after the baby. The women worked hard trying to do their own chores and seeing to the crops and animals as well. It was a sore struggle for them. Not a word did they hear of the battle on the mainland.

One evening as the days were getting shorter, Máire went as usual to see to Don Antonio's meal. He was in a very odd mood that evening. He was living in his cabin as the weather had got cold and twice he had left his meal to go to the door and look out over the ocean. Each time he asked Máire to make again the promise that she had made several years before. Máire was surprised and disturbed. Don Antonio had never mentioned the promise in all those years and she had often wondered if he had forgotten it.

Her friend ate very little of his meal that evening and, as she made her way back to her cabin, Máire found herself worrying about him. The night was getting more and more wild. She stopped for a moment, staring at the Atlantic. The waves were white-topped and the sky was an angry purple. She shivered and drew her blanket closer around her. Just then a whirling flock of seagulls swarmed up from the cliffs and wheeled above Don Antonio's cabin. Their cry was the loneliest and most pitiful she had ever heard. It spoke of grief and tragedy, of death and mourning.

Máire remembered evenings in happier times when people gathered round the firesides and told stories to while away the winter evenings. She remembered an old woman telling her once when she was very young that when men were drowned at sea and their bodies never found, then their lost souls became seagulls. And they cried and wept until the great gods of the sea had mercy on them and took them beyond the western ocean where they would live for ever in a land of beauty and plenty.

This was the night that Conor MacFadden chose to carry out his evil plan. If he waited any longer then the winter would be upon them and he might never escape from the island. Already the first storm was brewing. He watched as Máire left Don Antonio's cabin and waited until he was sure she was safely back in her own home. Then, throwing away the stick that he had been using as a crutch, he crept slowly towards the stranger's cabin. A flock of seagulls was swirling above the thatched roof and when he drew near they set up such a racket that he thought Don Antonio would surely come out to see what was happening, but the door remained closed.

He leaned his shoulder against the door, gave a mighty push and it flew open, tumbling him into the small room. Don Antonio sat on a stool facing the door. He did not seem in the least surprised by his late visitor. Conor felt the man was sitting there waiting for him.

"Where is the gold?" he shouted, waving the knife he used to gut fish. "If you do not give it to me I will kill you." Don Antonio simply turned his eyes towards a hollow in the wall and there lay the pouch and the treasure.

"You are going to kill me anyway," said Don Antonio, "but that doesn't matter. I am ready to go. I wish to be with my crew at last."

Conor didn't understand a word of Spanish but he could see that the man showed no fear. This puzzled and angered him. He shouted at Don Antonio but he did not reply. He shouted again and sent the wooden dishes on he table clattering to the floor.

The man smiled. "A coward always needs to make noise," he said in perfect Irish.

The insult was enough to send Conor MacFadden into a wild and murderous rage.

Máire was in a strange mood when she returned to the cabin. Her mother could not understand why she kept going to the door and staring over in the direction of Don Antonio's cabin. She could not possibly see it from the door.

"You are very restless, Máire," she said. "Come in and

shut the door. The wind is getting up and it is cold."

Máire could not content herself. She knew that something dreadful was about to happen. The wind told her, the seagulls told her and the look she had seen in Don Antonio's eyes had told her. She could stand it no longer,

"Something is wrong up there, Mother," she said, "and I will not be able sit in peace until I find out."

Leaving her baby daughter in her grandmother's charge, she went out once again into the darkness of the night.

The wind tore at her blanket as she climbed the hill but she battled against it as it stole the breath from her. Don Antonio's cabin was built in the shelter of a large rock, facing the Atlantic and the spot where his ship had foundered.

When she reached the crest of the hill and looked down, Máire knew immediately that she was right. Something terrible had happened. The door of the cabin was open and swinging crazily in the wind. She ran on, terrified of what she might find. The cabin was empty and the rush light spluttered in the draught. Her heart sank. She was sure Don Antonio had not waited for death to take him: he had gone to the clifftop and thrown himself into the sea. Again she heard the plaintive cry of the gulls above the moan of the wind. Then she noticed the blood on the floor.

Frantically she rushed out into the night. She strained to listen against the noise of the gulls and the wind and then she heard it: the clink of metal against stone. It came from a flat patch to the side of the house just above the cliffs. At first she could see nothing and then the full moon slipped out from behind a cloud and she saw the whole dreadful scene.

Conor MacFadden was shovelling as if a monster from Hell were after his soul. He had dug a long trench, a grave, and in it lay the body of the man who had been a father to her for ten years.

"What have you done, Conor MacFadden?" she screamed in despair. But he did not hear her. He went on throwing soil over the body. She ran forward and pulled his arm. He swirled round, knocking her to the ground.

"Máire, he wouldn't give me the gold," he lied as he bent to lift her to her feet, "so I had to kill him. Don't you see, Máire? He is only a stranger. We have had nothing but bad luck since he came to the island. Come away with me, Máire. With the gold we can live in comfort in a fine house."

"Go away with you! You have killed a gentle man who never did you any harm. A man I loved like a father—and you ask me to go away with you!"

"There is nothing for you here any longer, Máire. Come with me and be my wife."

"I am a wife — a wife to a brave man who has nothing but honour and love in his heart. You are eaten with greed and hatred. I wouldn't go with you if you gave me the queen of England's throne."

The loathing and disgust in Máire's eyes told Conor that she would never willingly be his. He was never a steady young man, and once he had murdered he had lost any trace of sanity. The rage boiled up in him.

"You will never see your brothers or your husband again!" he shouted. "I know Owen MacSweeney's plans. There is to be a great battle against the English. I know what castles he hides in. The English will pay well for this knowledge and Owen MacSweeney and his fine warriors will pay with their lives. And you will come with me or die."

The mad gleam in his eye and the froth bubbling from his mouth told Máire that Conor MacFadden was beyond pleading with. She had to find some way to stop him or the men of the island would be slaughtered. First she had to save herself. She had to get away from the insane man before she could do anything to help the others.

She ran. Blindly she sped, slipping and sliding in the darkness. Her lungs were bursting and her heart was hammering. Conor was strong and she could hear his rasping breath behind her. She called aloud for help but there was no one to hear her. Then she stumbled on a jutting rock. She was upright in a moment but Conor's strong arm was round her neck. She struggled like a wild animal in a trap but he was choking the breath from her. They twisted and turned, Máire kicked and punched. In the struggle they had edged closer to the cliff. The seagulls were now screaming above their heads. They darted and dived, their sharp beaks stabbing at Conor's ears, his cheeks, his eyes, the hand that gripped Máire's throat. He tried to beat off the attack and relaxed his grip.

Máire broke loose but he was after her and caught the streaming tail of her cloak. He pulled her to him and she scratched and kicked. The gulls screeched and dabbed with their dagger-sharp beaks. Conor lost his footing and stumbled to the ground, pulling his victim on top of him. Máire felt a cold sharp pain in her side and then a warm sticky gush. Conor pushed the limp form away and stood up staring in horror at his knife. It dripped dark and deadly in the pale moonlight.

Shocked at what he had done, he stepped back. The cliff edge crumbled and he slid screaming into the emptiness. The seagulls accompanied him on his last journey down into the open arms of the black waters.

The pain in Máire's side was dull and she was weak from loss of blood. She groped around trying to get herself to her feet and her hand felt the soft leather of Don Antonio's pouch. It was heavy but she tied it round her waist and clawed her way back to the body of her friend. With what strength she had left she placed the pouch in the grave, covered Don Antonio's body with the cut sods and covered the mound with small stones that were scattered all around. Then, slowly and painfully, she dragged herself home.

Máire's mother cared for her and tended her wound but it would not heal and she got weaker every day. Each evening, at twilight, she could hear the wailing of the seagulls above Carraig Rua and she thought of the broken body of Don Antonio in his cold grave in the bog. Máire knew that she would never be able to keep the solemn promise she had made to her homesick friend; someone else would have to do that.

Having seen the power of greed, Máire felt she could trust no one but her mother with the secret of Don Antonio's grave. But the old woman was too frail to take on the burden of the promise, and little María was too young. In the weeks that followed that tragic night, Máire told her mother the story and the whereabouts of the grave. The old woman listened to every word so that she in turn could tell her granddaughter when she was old enough to understand. The golden cross would be young María's inheritance and with it would go the promise that her mother had made. She would be in honour bound to see that the remains of Don Antonio Serralles were removed from Inishbwee and buried at sea. If she could not fulfil her mother's promise then the cross and the obligation must be passed on until a kinswoman of the MacSweeney clan would succeed where Máire MacGinley had failed.

Gradually Máire began to slip away from all that she loved and one night, she kissed her baby and died peacefully in her mother's arms.

It was a terrible time in Ireland then. After a great victory in the north against the English, the chieftains had marched south to meet a fleet of ships that had sailed from Spain to help them in their struggle. When they reached Kinsale in County Cork, the chieftains discovered that a battle was in full swing between the English and the Spanish soldiers. The Spaniards were having a hard time of it and they withdrew. The great Irish earls were defeated.

They returned home but they feared for their lives and so they decided to sail away into exile. Many of the smaller chieftains went with them and among them was Owen MacSweeney. The earls and the chieftains left Donegal and sailed for Europe in the year 1607 and five years later Owen MacSweeney died in Spain, longing for his home in the beautiful island of Inishbwee. He was buried there in a foreign land, the homeland of Don Antonio, and far across the sea, his friend lay uneasily in the soil of Inishbwee.

The story that had kept Eimear enthralled for an hour had been written many years after the tragic events. In the years following the sad Flight of the Earls, Inishbwee had suffered great disturbance and the exact location of the Spaniard's grave had been lost. The story, however, had been passed down through generations of women who, although they had taken their husbands' names, had carried the blood of the MacSweeney clan. With the story went the promise and the golden cross.

The tiny words in the old-fashioned language were written by one who had possession of the cross but had been unable to keep the promise because she did not know the whereabouts of the grave. She finished the story with a strange prophecy.

Don Antonio Serralles would rest undisturbed in the black peat of the island until he was threatened once again by greed. Then the spirit of Máire MacGinley would search for a kinswoman to whom she would reveal the secret of the Spaniard's grave. That kinswoman would be bound by the solemn promise made centuries ago and she would return the lonely sea-captain to the wild ocean and the arms of his countrymen.

The story finished with a poem, a lament of sorrow for Ireland after its chiefs had gone to live in foreign lands:

> Her chiefs are gone. There's none to bear
> Her cross or lift her from despair.
> The grieving lords take ship. With these
> Our very lords pass overseas.

Man after man, day after day
Her noblest princes pass away
And leave all the rabble rest
A land dispeopled of her best.

Slowly Eimear put down the papers. The light was failing now. She looked out to Inishbwee. The sun was setting over the island and it was of such beauty that she caught her breath in wonder. The great orange orb set the sky on fire and turned the water to molten gold. Inishbwee stood out in stark outline against the fiery glow, black and brooding and empty.

❦ ❦ ❦

7

Eimear's Inheritance

Eimear tossed and turned all night and the night you don't sleep very well is a night filled with dreams. Eimear's dreams were jumbled and confused and very disturbing. In one she was hanging on by her fingertips to the smooth edge of a precipice. Unseen hands prised her fingers loose and she went tumbling into a black abyss.

She awoke with a start, relieved to be safe under her quilt. Then she climbed out of bed and made an effort to get washed and dressed. She knew she had to see Ban Nolan as soon as possible to return the papers. She wasn't sorry for stealing the folder from the Black Diver but she still felt like a thief.

"You look a bit tired this morning, Eimear," said Nan. "Did the story give you nightmares?"

Eimear choked on her porridge. "What story?" she stammered.

"The story you went to bed early to read, the book you said you were dying to finish."

"Oh, yes," said Eimear relieved. "Yea, it was great."

Then to get the subject away from her bedtime reading she said, "I'll collect the milk this morning, Nan."

Ban Nolan seemed to be waiting for Eimear. She was sitting outside her door with cats on her knee and cats curled round her feet. The geese were picking at corn scattered on the bare patch of ground around her chair, and after giving Eimear a fierce look they went on about their business.

"Sit down, Eimear," said the old woman in her soft voice. There was a three-legged stool beside her and Eimear settled herself on it.

"It was nice of you to come to see me this morning."

Guiltily, Eimear handed her the blue folder.

"What's in that?" Ban Nolan asked mildly.

"Your papers, the ones that were on your table."

Ban Nolan nodded her head and smiled. Eimear was sure she knew exactly what was in the folder.

Then an anxious thought struck her. "I didn't steal them," she said quickly and then more slowly added, "At least I didn't steal them from you."

"You didn't steal them at all," said Ban Nolan. "You can't steal what's yours already."

Eimear hadn't the foggiest notion what the old woman meant. "Mine?" she asked, puzzled.

"Yes, yours." There was a pause and Ban Nolan raised her head and looked all around her, as if she were gathering her thoughts from the hedges.

"It is time," she said finally. "You have the MacSweeney blood in you, Eimear Kelly. I have had the inheritance too long. It belongs to you now. As it was passed on to me I now pass it to you."

Eimear's heart was thumping wildly. She took back the folder, placed it on her knees and folded her trembling hands over it. Ban Nolan's speckled brown hand covered her own short plump hands. Eimear looked up at the old woman.

"And remember, Eimear," the soft voice dropped and became more urgent, "with those papers goes the promise. That too is yours now. For four hundred years no one has been able to keep that promise because no one knows exactly where the Spanish captain lies buried. At least during that time he lay undisturbed, but now there is a change. Greed once again is tearing at Inishbwee and I am too old to do anything about it. The job is yours now, Eimear, but you must be very careful. Greed is powerful. It will stop at nothing until it is satisfied."

Although the sun was already warm Eimear felt cold. She wanted to tell Ban Nolan that she was a daft old woman and wandering in her mind; that the story in the folder was nonsense and nothing to do with her. She didn't say a word. She rose from the low stool and walked towards the lane. When she got there she turned round but the chair was empty. A huge Siamese cat had eased herself into it and she stared at Eimear with an eye as blue as Ban Nolan's.

Kate listened, holding her breath as Eimear told her the story of the Spanish captain and the buried treasure. Even Ronan stopped labelling his jars to listen. She didn't tell them the whole story. She left out the part about the promise being handed down and what had happened at Ban Nolan's house.

"So that is why the Black Diver is digging on Inishbwee," breathed Kate. "He's looking for the grave and the pouch of gold and jewels." All the children, even the twins, were now using Eimear's name for the unpleasant man now living in their old holiday home.

"If he is, he's breaking the law," said Ronan. "Treasure trove belongs to the country and if he finds anything and doesn't hand it over then he will be charged. I think we should get the gardaí in on this.

"Oh, no!" cried Eimear. "We have no proof of anything, only an old superstition. They would just laugh at us."

She had no idea how she was going to stop the Black Diver or keep Máire MacGinley's promise but she knew that gardaí tramping round Inishbwee would be no help at all.

"I suppose you're right," said Ronan. "We need to get over to Inishbwee and spy on him. When we have some solid information then we can go to the gardaí."

"Yes," said Eimear eagerly. "I'll ask Nan if we can have *Báidín* tomorrow."

More than anything Eimear wanted to get to Inishbwee. She hoped that once she was on the island something or someone would tell her what to do. That night she made plans. Tomorrow they would take a picnic and spend the whole day on Inishbwee.

❦ ❦ ❦

8

The Shadow

Well, you know what usually happens when you make plans—something always makes a mess of them. Eimear's plans were no exception. The weather, which had been beautiful for a fortnight, turned very bad indeed. The whole world seemed wrapped in a sodden spongy layer of drooping grey clouds. Dragged down by their watery weight, the clouds flopped over hilltops and slid down into valleys, making it impossible to see clearly on land or sea.

Just to make conditions even more miserable, a westerly gale swept in from the Atlantic, bending the trees so that they bowed to the east like devout Muslims at prayer, and driving the rain with the force of a power-drill into unprotected faces.

In weather like this it is impossible to go out in a boat, and islands along the coast can be cut off for weeks. So, although Eimear was burning to get over to Inishbwee she had to settle herself and wait until the weather did the same.

No boats could survive on the stormy seas, so the Black Diver was grounded too, and that was a comfort to Eimear.

The children, however, didn't let the rain spoil their holidays. They exchanged swimsuits for wellies and rain-gear and found things to do. Ronan Farrelly had received a letter from his girl-friend telling him what a boring, miserable time she was having in Belfast without him and this had cheered him up immensely. He became a member of the human race again and he organised fishing trips and bird-watching expeditions or led the others as they padded through bogs collecting specimens for his science project. When they were indoors the children played cards, Scrabble or Monopoly in the caravan or in Nan's sitting-room. All the time, however, Eimear's mind was on Inishbwee and she itched to get over there. But the rain continued to pour and the winds to howl.

The nearest town to Magherabeg is Dungloe and at the end of every month of July they have a festival. It is called the Mary of Dungloe festival and it culminates in the choosing of a young woman to be that year's "Mary." There are many festival events besides, and Dungloe dedicates itself to the business of having a good time. Locals and visiting holiday-makers look forward eagerly to the she-nanigans. Mr Farrelly arranged a trip to the festival and of course Eimear and Nan Sweeney were included. It was just as well the Farrellys had a very old, but very roomy, estate car: otherwise they would never all have fitted in,

"I wonder will the swingboats be there this year," burbled Kate, "and Francie Future."

Francie was an old man who travelled the length and

breadth of Ireland following fairs and festivals. His means of transport was an ancient motor-cycle and trailer. He was half magician and half fortune-teller. The trailer was packed with tattered scarves and feather flowers, balloons and fake rabbits, dolls and dummies as old and battered as himself. With these Francie would weave tales that kept children of all ages spellbound for hours.

Francie *was* there and the swingboats and the street musicians who entertained the crowd from every free space on a pavement. The main street was decorated with bunting and crowds surged along, weaving in and out of shops, pubs and cafés. There were jugglers and clowns who painted the children's faces, a mime artist and a puppet-show. Kilted pipe bands marched in their gold-and-green costumes and the steel tips on the buckled, patent leather shoes of the dancers tapped out reels and jigs on the boards of tractor trailers.

Eimear and Kate and Ronan were free to roam by themselves as the three adults looked after the twins and the baby. They scurried from one feature to the next, afraid that they would miss something good at the next stall.

They rushed about so much that of course they lost each other in the milling crowds. Eimear wasn't bothered. Dungloe hasn't too many streets and she knew that she would meet everybody at the festival at least three times. She bought herself an ice-cream cone and wandered happily at a slower pace. Although the sky was grey and the streets were wet there was a lull in the rain and so she lowered the hood of her anorak.

After a while she noticed that she no longer felt as

carefree as before. She was uneasy. She felt she was being followed. She wanted out of the crowded street. The throngs of people with their strings of balloons and sticky toddlers on shoulders seemed to be closing in on her. She began to move more quickly through the crowd. Children are very good at doing this. They can slip sideways through the tiniest spaces and worm their way round any obstacle.

Soon Eimear was standing under the last string of bunting at the edge of the crowd and she felt much better. The low wall of a bridge stretched on one side of the street and she sat down on it for a few minutes. She looked back up the street just to make sure that no one *had* followed her. Then she walked down a narrow lane between the houses towards a rocky, seaweed-covered beach. It wasn't a sitting-around beach but it was a great place for skimming stones.

Eimear hunted until she had a good collection of flat stones. She chose the best, hooked her finger and thumb round it and sent it flying over the water with a strong underarm throw. It hit the surface and then bounced up again to continue its journey. One, two, three, four, five, six times it bounced. That was a good throw. She competed against herself until she used up her pile of stones but she never managed to do better than that first throw.

A fine mizzle was drifting in from the sea and Eimear, deciding it was time to find Kate and Ronan again, turned away from the shore. There at the entrance to the lane, with his back to Eimear, stood the Black Diver. Her escape route was blocked! Crouching over, she ran to hide behind a rusted oil-drum that was collecting rain water from the spoutings of one of the houses.

The position allowed Eimear a clear view of the man's actions and even if he turned and looked down the lane she was sure she would be out of his sight. What was he doing there? Had he been following her? The man was looking up and down as if he didn't know which direction to turn. Then he pulled up the hood of his anorak against the drizzle and moved off across the street. Eimear decided that it was her turn to do a bit of following.

The Black Diver walked slowly along the main street. He stopped at a corner, took a newspaper from his pocket, checked something in it and, satisfied that he had found the street he was looking for, walked briskly down the line of terraced houses, coming to a halt at the fourth house down. Again he checked the paper, nodded in satisfaction and knocked at the door. Eimear was too far away to hear what the Black Diver said to the man who answered the door. It was short, whatever it was, and the two disappeared quickly indoors and closed the door.

"There you are, we've been looking for you everywhere. It's time to go home."

Kate and Ronan seemed to be a bit annoyed with her as they came panting out of the festivities.

"I can't go yet," she said.

"What do you mean, can't?" Kate was definitely annoyed. "Mammy and Daddy are in the car, the baby is yowling and your Nan is trying to keep the twins from murdering each other."

"What're you doing here anyway?" asked Ronan.

"Keep back," said Eimear. "Get in behind me. It's the Black Diver; he's gone into that house and if he comes out he'll see you."

She elbowed them round the corner and all three heads fought for room to squint round the edge of the wall. She was just in time. At that moment the door of the house opened and the two men stood chatting. Then they shook hands and the Black Diver moved in their direction. He was carrying something. Something with a very long handle.

"It's a metal detector!" said Ronan.

"Quick, back to the car before he sees us," squeaked Eimear.

The three of them scampered off and didn't look back until they were safely packed into the back of the car.

"I can just guess what he is going to do with that metal detector," Kate whispered hotly. "Maybe we *should* tell the gardaí."

"There is no crime in owning a metal detector," Ronan answered. "It isn't even a crime to use it. But if anything old and valuable is found and it is not turned over to the state, then that is a crime."

"We'll have to watch every move he makes," Eimear decided. "The minute the weather improves he will be off to Inishbwee looking for the Spanish gold, and we must be right behind him."

❦ ❦ ❦

9

Things Get Out of Hand

For the next four days the rain poured and lashed, and lashed and poured. Now and again a watery sun peeped from behind windswept clouds, and spirits rose. But the god of the weather was only having his little joke and as soon as deckchairs were out and barbecues lit the demon returned, joyfully dousing fires with splurges of drenching rain and uprooting deckchairs and table-umbrellas with the playfulness of a ferocious lion.

Kate, Ronan and Eimear were out in all weathers trying to keep an eye on the Black Diver. It was fun at first lying in boggy hollows with the binoculars trained on his cottage and the rain wiping out any view they might have had; they felt they were doing something exciting and sort of Sherlock-Holmesy. But then they got a bit fed up. Rain is cold even in the summertime, and when nothing at all happened the spying seemed a bit silly. And indeed it *was* silly. They only had to check that the Black Diver's rubber boat was still pulled up on the grass above the beach to be sure that he hadn't risked the storm and sneaked off to the island. So, after a day or two of playing detective the thrill wore off and they contented themselves with checking on the boat.

Even children do at times get a bit browned off with bad weather, and Eimear and the Farrelly children had reached that point. The adult Farrellys had reached it long ago. Keeping five children occupied and separating them when tempers boil and a riot threatens is a very difficult task—especially in a caravan.

Nan Sweeney could see that the grown-up Farrellys needed a break and the children could do with a bit of excitement.

"No, I insist," she said in such a way that it was no use arguing with her. "Isn't it your wedding anniversary? You'll never get the chance again. There's singing and dancing and supper laid on and sure you might as well take advantage of the cheap offer."

Mr and Mrs Farrelly were tempted. The local hotel, in an effort to fill empty bedrooms, was running a night of entertainment with evening meal and bed and breakfast at a very reasonable price. "Go on o'r that," said Nan, making their minds up for them. "Sure I'll stay over here with the wee ones and the older two can stay in the cottage with Eimear. They can't get up to any divilment that I won't know about."

It was great fun making all the arrangements. The twins were delighted as Nan Sweeney told the best stories they had ever heard and didn't get one bit annoyed no matter how many times they got out of bed to look for a drink of water. Kate and Ronan brought their sleeping-bags over to the cottage and prepared to have a night of fun.

Nan had left loads of food so they planned a midnight feast. They couldn't have the lights on at that time or Nan would be over tapping at the window so Ronan brought his very powerful torch. The two girls were supposed to sleep in Eimear's room and Ronan in Nan's but after they had eaten enough to gorge five elephants and told the scariest stories they could remember, Ronan preferred to curl up in his sleeping-bag on the soft rug on the floor of Eimear's bedroom.

It was almost midnight before the trio drifted off into the deep sleep that comes when you have tired yourself out having fun, and they would have slept well into the middle of the next day if something hadn't probed and picked at Eimear's brain, coaxing it awake.

Too much of Nan's apple-tart, she thought as she turned over on her stomach and tried to get back to sleep. There was a throbbing in her ears that would not let her settle. She wondered if they had left the portable radio on. The sound would not go away. Fully awake now, she sat up. The sound was coming from outside the room and now that her mind was working properly she knew exactly what it was. It was the outboard engine of a boat.

She leapt out of bed and over to the window. In the night the wind had settled and now the sea was calm and brightly lit by a full moon. A small boat carved a white-foamed V in the still water. Although she knew in her heart and soul it was the Black Diver she had to make sure it was not some fisherman before she disturbed Kate and Ronan.

Flinging on her dressing-gown and taking Ronan's torch, Eimear quietly left the cottage and tiptoed past the shed where the dogs were sleeping. She needn't have worried. The three collies were the worst watchdogs in the world. They were very noisy and active during the day but at night they liked to snuggle up together and dream of great flocks of sheep waiting to be shepherded away from danger.

She flew across the grass and down the steps onto the beach. The rubber boat was gone! From the rocks to the water's edge the sand was flattened and scooped between two ridges, like the trail left by a giant sea-slug.

"Wake up," Eimear urged, shaking her friends in turn. "Come on you two: we need to move."

"Oh Mammy, I'm sick. Can I not stay home today?" Kate mumbled, thinking she was getting up for school.

"Eejit!" hissed Eimear, whipping the pillow from under Kate's head and thumping Ronan with it.

"We can't go without telling your Nan." Ronan had listened to Eimear's frantic appeals to get into *Báidín* and go after the Black Diver and he was being, "the only person present with a titter of common sense." Eimear felt like giving him a good shaking.

"And if we *do* go over there and tell her, what will she say?" she demanded hotly. "I'll tell you what she'll say. She'll say the man has a perfect right to go out in his boat at one o'clock in the morning and if we don't get back to bed before the wee ones wake, she'll roast our backsides. That's what she'll say."

"Oh, come on, Ronan," urged Kate. "It'll be a bit of fun

and sure there's no danger. The sea's as flat as a pancake now. Don't be such a scaredy-cat."

"Whether you're coming or not, I'm going," said Eimear. By this time she had pulled on her jeans and a warm jumper and her wellies and anorak and was out the door on her way to the beach. Kate, hauling on her clothes, was close behind her. They thought Ronan wasn't coming as he was ages joining them on the beach.

"Afraid you might miss something?" teased Kate when she saw him coming down the steps. She was right: Ronan *was* afraid he might miss something and also he didn't like the suggestion that he was a bit of a coward.

The girls were struggling with *Báidín* and he felt they were in need of his manly strength.

"Here, you need to get your shoulder under it," he said, shoving Eimear aside. He hunched himself to pit his might against the small boat and it shot into the water, leaving Ronan flat on his face on the sand. Kate let out a small hoot of laughter and Eimear had to stifle her own giggles in case they woke Nan. The three waded until the boat was floating and then they pulled themselves aboard and put on their life-jackets.

They didn't use the outboard engine on the journey to Inishbwee. Although it was slower to row and tough on the arms, they didn't want to warn the Black Diver that they were on their way.

Ahead the island loomed black against the pale sky and silvery sea. As they neared the shore the three grew silent. What was waiting for them on Inishbwee? Eimear knew that before she took her leave of the island something would happen to her, something very strange and very frightening.

10

The Ferny Hollow

Báidín slipped quietly onto the tiny beach and the three children hurriedly pulled it up into the grass and hid her among the whin bushes. They stripped off their life-jackets and stored them underneath the seats. There was no sign of the rubber boat.

"He could have landed anywhere," said Ronan. "Those rubber boats come right up the beach and they're very easily hidden."

"What do we do now?" asked Kate, shoving her hands into her pockets to warm them.

"We have to establish base camp," said Ronan, preparing to take charge of the expedition. Boys usually do try to take charge and they can be fairly good at it.

"Somewhere dry and sheltered," he went on, but he was talking to himself. Eimear was already leading the way to the deserted village and Kate was hot on her heels.

"Yes, I think this will do nicely," he panted, arriving

breathless at the cottage in which Eimear and her Nan had spent the night. Eimear was already shaking out the pile of ferns they had left behind them on that occasion. The top ones were badly withered but those underneath were still fresh enough to cover them and provide a little heat.

"There isn't much we can do until daylight," she said. "If we use the torch he'll see us and come after us."

"We should try to get some sleep now so that we are good and fresh in the morning. Then we'll see what the Black Diver is up to," decided Ronan. They huddled together for warmth under the ferns and soon they were unconscious, exhausted after their midnight feast and the hard pulling on the oars.

Eimear must have dozed for a couple of hours, for when she woke the dawn was streaking the sky with a watery light. She lay with her eyes wide open, staring out the door. A flash of light in the distance alarmed her. She knew it was from the torch of the Black Diver, and the beam was coming from the direction of Carraig Rua.

She rose from her bed of ferns and went to stand in the doorway. The weather had changed again and although it was not raining, the wind was chasing clouds across the sky and tossing the whins like feather-dusters. In the dim light she could just about see the length of the overgrown street to where the land sloped up towards the wildest part of the island and the site of the ruined castle that was perched on the edge of the treacherous cliffs. At the top of the slope there was a patch darker than the surrounding gloom. It was not a still, dense patch. It flowed and swirled as if it had life and purpose.

The movement curled and twisted and Eimear was drawn towards it. She left the shelter of her doorway and walked slowly to the foot of the slope. She looked up. The dark patch was beginning to take shape: it was no longer traily and vapoury—it was becoming more solid. Eimear found herself looking up into the face of a young woman, the same face she had seen on her last visit to Inishbwee.

Again the girl was troubled and seemed to be asking for help. She was wrapped in a thick blanket and her wide skirt billowed around her bare feet.

"Who are you?" whispered Eimear, although she knew the answer.

The girl did not appear to speak but Eimear could hear a voice in her head saying, "Eimear Kelly, kinswoman of the MacSweeneys, my promise is yours now. When Don Antonio Serralles is at peace, then I, too, will find rest. Eimear of the MacSweeneys, come follow me."

Máire MacGinley was gone.

"Wait!" called Eimear. "Wait for me. I'm coming!"

The wind was now as fierce as ever it had been before the earlier calm of the night, and large raindrops were splattering the bare rocks. Although the light was still weak, Eimear had no difficulty following the white feet of the girl as she tripped from rock to rock. On and on they ran towards Carraig Rua, and Eimear battled against the streaming wind. She had a pain in her throat that burned right down into her lungs.

At last Máire MacGinley came to a stop and Eimear knew exactly where she was. She had been here before with Nan Sweeney and now she knew why she had had that strange feeling that something was drawing her like a magnet into the heart of the ferny hollow.

It was the wind that woke Kate. It came howling in through the door and the hole in the roof, rustling the ferns and making her shiver. "Eimear," she whispered when she saw the empty space beside her. "Eimear!"

Fear clutched at her heart when she realised that her friend was no longer in the cottage. There are parts of Inishbwee that are not safe even on the sunniest of days and Eimear was out there in a gathering storm in the half-light.

"Ronan!" she called in her panic, "Eimear's gone!"

They checked outside in case Eimear had just gone for a walk. They didn't shout for her, afraid that their calls might tell the Black Diver that they were on the island.

"Stupid!" said Ronan angrily. "She, of all people, knows how dangerous it is to wander off on her own. She didn't take the torch either, so she can hardly have seen where she was going."

"But where *was* she going?" asked Kate.

"I dunno. After the Black Diver I suppose. She should have waited for us. She'll ruin everything! What is she going to do if she *does* find him and he *has* dug up some treasure? Ask him politely to hand it over or she'll tell on him?"

"Ever since she read those papers," Kate said thoughtfully, "she's been a bit odd about this whole thing, as if it was her own special mission or something. In fact she's been strange since the first day we went to Ban Nolan's cottage." Kate was not just worried about Eimear; she was hurt that her friend had gone off without her.

"I don't think she told us the whole story about those papers and I bet that old bat has filled her head with stories and superstitions," said Ronan, getting as annoyed as Kate.

"We'll have to *do* something," said Kate as she paced up and down the street trying to keep her balance in the wind. "The weather is getting worse and she might be in danger."

"I'm glad now I left that note," said Ronan.

"What note?"

"The note I wrote to Eimear's Nan before I left the cottage."

"So that's what kept you," said Kate with interest. "What did you say?"

"I said we were going over to Inishbwee after the Black Diver, who was going to steal the buried treasure belonging to a captain of the Spanish Armada."

"Oh."

"Sounds a bit daft, doesn't it?"

"Mammy and Daddy won't believe it," said Kate. "They'll just let us stay here until the storm dies down. Then they'll tell us that a good starving should have put the crazy notions out of us."

"Yeah, you're right," mumbled Ronan gloomily. "Even if they did believe even a wee bit of the story, they couldn't take a boat out in that weather."

"Well, what's the plan then?" Kate wanted to cry. She was cold and hungry and very afraid.

"We go and look for Eimear," said Ronan, putting a comforting arm round her, "and see if she needs any help."

11

Panic Stations

At that precise moment Eimear was about to enter the ferny hollow. The ghostly figure of Máire MacGinley had vanished. She had brought Eimear to the hollow and now she left her to solve the mystery as best she could. She looked around her and realised that she must be on or near the very spot where the Spaniard's cabin had once been. The ferns had grown since then, hiding any traces of house or grave.

Her heart was thumping painfully but Eimear forced herself to enter the boggy jungle. It closed around her, clawing at her hair and face. She felt as if a heavy weight had been placed on her chest and she could barely breathe. On she went, not knowing in which direction she was travelling. The ferns closed in above her head and she couldn't see the sky. The wind was battering the ferns from above but, strangely, Eimear felt none of its force.

She had gone hardly any distance at all when she felt

again the strange pull into the thick green heart of the hollow. This time, although the ground was even wetter than before, her feet did not sink into the boggy muck. Instead she glided over the swamp as if her sturdy body weighed less than a ball of bog-cotton.

The ferns no longer tried to block her way. They swayed apart, opening a pathway for her and guiding her in the direction they wished her to go. She knew she had reached her destination when she fell over it!

In the centre of the hollow a grassy mound rose up from the swamp, and Eimear now lay sprawled on it. The centre of the hollow was free of ferns and the pale cold light of the dawn streamed down on her. Eimear had to think what to do next. Was this the grave of Don Antonio de Seralles?

Around her on the grass were scattered several small moss-covered stones. She chose the sharpest and began to scrape at the grass on the top of the mound. At first she seemed to make no progress at all. Then a sod came free and she dug at the softer underclay. There was a rasp of stone against stone. She scraped on and soon she had uncovered an area as large as a dinner plate. She was certain now that she had found the layer of stones that Máire MacGinley had placed on her friend's grave almost four hundred years before. The stones were firmly embedded in the sticky soil. It would take her hours to dig them out and then she had to find some way to get whatever remained of Don Antonio back to the ocean.

"I'll do it somehow," she vowed. "Ronan and Kate will help me and somehow we will return the Spanish captain to his ship and crew."

"Well, well!"

The shock of the booming voice behind her made Eimear slip off the mound, and she landed on her bottom beside a muddy pair of black wellington boots. She looked up into the grinning face of the Black Diver!

The man was not a pleasant sight to see. His beard and hair were tangled and matted with dirt and his dark jacket was smeared with trails of drying muck. He was carrying a spade and the metal detector he had bought in Dungloe.

"I had a notion that if I followed you I might find something interesting."

"Y…y…you have no business here," stammered Eimear. "This place has nothing to do with you."

"It has a lot to do with me," the man said, smiling. "I spent months reading about the route of the Spanish Armada and working out the most likely spot on this coast to find a wreck. There are loads of them still undiscovered, you know. All round the west coast. They're sitting down there covered in green slime and every year that passes they rot a little more. But gold doesn't rot. Gold comes to no harm at all in salt water."

He had moved forward a little while he was talking and stuck his spade into the ground. "I was certain there was a wreck on the north side of Inishbwee," he said, lifting his metal detector, "but I dived over every square inch of the sea bottom and came up zero. I was about to give up and go home and then one night, when I was sitting in a pub, I heard the legend of the Spanish captain. Stupid nonsense, I thought. But then again, I thought, sure I might as well find out."

By this time he had switched on the detector and was sweeping the base of the mound with the round flat head.

"They said that that old bag of bones in the cottage near me knew something about it; that the secret had been passed down to her in some old papers from her great-great-grandmother or something. Rubbish! I said to myself. But still, there was no harm in having a look. The papers were there all right, just waiting for somebody to pick them up. And there on the wall was a picture of a lassie wearing a fine cross. A cross almost identical to one that had been found ten years ago on a Spanish wreck on the north coast." The metal detector had covered all the flat area around the mound without raising a single bleep.

"Those papers made interesting reading too—as long as I got keeping them. Some little sneak-thief crept into my cottage and made off with them. If ever I get my hands on him—or her—that'll be one very, very sorry person."

At this he turned and looked at Eimear and the threat in the black eyes sent a cold chill through her.

"Well, never mind, I told myself, I knew all I needed to know, except the exact spot where the Spaniard was buried—and no one knows that."

He pulled a packet of cigarettes from his pocket, lit one, inhaled deeply and blew the smoke in Eimear's direction.

"So I came over here in the dead of night with my little magic wand to make my fortune. I dug and I dug all over this blasted island and did I find anything? Yes, indeed I did. I found baked-bean tins and three-legged pots and even a holy medal, but not one thing did I find that would pay my expenses, never mind set me up for life."

He skited the butt of the cigarette with his thumb and it rose in an arc above the ferns before disappearing from sight.

"I was a bit downhearted, I might tell you," he said, resuming the search with the detector. "And then what should I see but little Miss Light-Fingers coming my way and she seemed to know exactly where she was going. And what do you know? She disappeared into the ferns. O-ho! says I to myself. There's a young lady worth watching. I will follow her and perhaps we will soon discover where the goodies lie buried."

A high-pitched bleep put an end to his speech. The sallow face of the man grew red with excitement. "Bingo!" he shouted and began to scrape frantically at the turf on the top of the mound.

Seeing him so distracted, Eimear began to shuffle on her bottom, backways, towards the ferns. All the time she kept a wary eye on the Black Diver. The effort of removing the top layer of sods was causing him to sweat a lot. She had to escape and get help before the grave was destroyed and the contents stolen. Her fingers, clawing the ground behind her, felt the first tough stalks of the ferns. She was almost there. Once she was in the tangle of leaves he would never find her, and she could get back to Ronan and Kate.

It was impossible to go through the jungle backways so she turned over on her tummy and began to slither forward. The man had his back to her and he was completely absorbed in his grave-robbing. She slid on. She was almost totally enveloped in the ferny fronds. She would get to her feet now and make a dash for it. She tried and fell flat on her face. Her foot was held in an iron grip!

"And where do you think you're going?"

The red face was thrust right into her own and she could smell the stink of tobacco on his breath.

"You sit right there, my lady, and perhaps if your mouth was stopped and there was a cord or two on your hands and feet, you might have a bit of manners."

As he spoke, he was pulling out the drawstring from the bottom of his anorak. Eimear was about to scream but her mouth was filled with woollen scarf. The thin cord bit into her wrists and ankles. The grave of Don Antonio de Serralles was about to be ransacked and she, Eimear Kelly— Eimear of the MacSweeneys—had led the thief straight to it!

❦ ❦ ❦

12

Big Wheels

Nan Sweeney didn't sleep very well when she was out of her own bed but she was so exhausted after telling story upon story to the twins and putting them back to bed five times that when she finally collapsed in the back bedroom of the caravan, she did fall into a very deep sleep indeed. It was the baby looking for her early morning bottle who jolted Nan out of her well-earned slumber.

The little face was looking at her through the bars of the cot, puzzled at seeing a strange face in her mammy and daddy's bed.

"Hello, my angel," said Nan. "It must be a terrible shock to see my wrinkled old face instead of your mammy's, but sure a bottle of milk tastes the same no matter who fills it."

She hooked the gurgling baby under her arm and went out to the kitchen to heat the milk. The twins were still sleeping in their bunk-room and Nan made as little noise as possible, as she had absolutely no wish to disturb those rascals. The baby had her bottle and then Nan gave her a plate of baby cereal. She plastered her own face and Nan's, her hair, her chair and finally the floor with the cereal. It is doubtful if any actually went into her mouth.

Nan eased the curtains back to let in some light and looked over at the cottage. There was no sign of activity but as it was only seven o'clock she didn't expect to see any. She also knew perfectly well that Eimear and her pals would have been at all sorts of carry-on until the early hours and wouldn't be opening an eye until near lunchtime. She would let them lie as long as they needed. She was disappointed that it wasn't a nice day; it had been so calm and dry when she was going to bed. But, no. The weather was up to its old tricks again and the children were as well in bed as out in the wind and rain.

To occupy herself, Nan bathed the baby in the kitchen sink and then she mopped up the flood. She dressed her and propped her up on some cushions on the floor with plenty of toys to keep her happy. She was just finished washing out some nappies and bibs when the door to the bunk-room flew open and she had to rescue the baby before she was trampled by the stampede. The awakening of the Farrelly twins was like the eruption of a ferocious volcano. The rearing of eleven children did not take as much out of Nan Sweeney as did the rest of that morning. For breakfast Josie wanted toast with cheese spread and strawberry jam and four sausages and Brendan wanted Rice Krispies with milk and honey and a spoonful of peanut butter. On his toast he demanded chocolate spread and potato crisps.

When the little dears were fed Nan thought it would be a good idea to get them out of doors, rain or no rain. But getting them dressed was another matter. Josie insisted on wearing her bikini, a blouse of her mother's and her own bright yellow plastic sandals. Brendan refused to get out of his pyjamas at all. Without entering into any arguments Nan pulled anoraks over their heads and put them out to dig in the pile of sand that had been carried up from the beach. She then released the dogs, sure that their delighted yelps would waken the snoring inhabitants of the cottage.

It was nearly eleven o'clock before the poor woman had the caravan cleared up and the baby back in her cot for a snooze. Grateful for a moment's rest, she sat down to have a cup of tea in peace and quiet. At any moment she expected to be summoned to the cottage to start breakfast there.

It was a wonder that the noise of the dogs and the squabbling of the twins, over identical buckets, hadn't already brought the sleepyheads to the door. Unease twitched at Nan like a dull toothache. Maybe she had better tiptoe to the cottage just to make sure that everything was all right.

She soon discovered that everything was *not* all right. A discarded sleeping-bag met her at the door and the bedclothes were tumbled on the bedroom floor. There was no sign of Eimear and the Farrellys. Could they have gone down to the beach earlier without Nan seeing them? No, that was impossible—and besides, they wouldn't have gone anywhere without breakfast. Something very odd had happened. Nan felt fear gnawing at her insides like a fat white maggot.

The note, perched high up on the mantelpiece beside

the picture of Granda Sweeney, went unnoticed until Nan was leaving the cottage and having a last look round in case she had missed anything. She lifted it down and read it slowly:

Dear Nan Sweeney,

We have gone to Inishbwee after Mr Diver. We believe that he is about to steal Spanish gold that belongs to the nation. Please tell my parents not to worry. We are perfectly all right. We will probably be back before you even read this letter.

Ronan Farrelly

PS I will look after the girls.

"The young eejit!" exploded Mr Farrelly when he read the note. "This comes from watching too much television. I thought Ronan had a bit of sense, that he'd grown out of the cops and robbers phase."

"Just look at the sea," worried Mrs Farrelly. "No boat could survive in that."

"Now don't be torturing yourself," comforted Nan. "They will have got over in perfect safety. The wind didn't get up until the morning."

"And they can stay there until it calms down a bit," stormed Mr Farrelly. "A good starving might teach them a lesson!"

He said this but he didn't really mean it. He too was worried and he was turning over in his mind ways and means of getting to the island.

"If they're not back in an hour," said Nan, "I'll see if one of the fishermen will try to get us over. Now you're not to be worrying," she added, putting an arm round Mrs

Farrelly. "It's all a bit of an adventure to them. They probably got themselves all steamed up with stories full of suspicious goings-on and now they're feeling a bit silly and very sorry for themselves. Eimear knows the island and they'll come to no harm."

In spite of her words, Nan Sweeney still had that nagging deep-in-the-pit-of-the-stomach feeling that everything was not as it should be. Being an islander herself, she had grown up with the legend of the Spanish captain, and she wondered if there was any truth in the children's suspicions about Mr William Diver. She hadn't liked the man from the first moment she set eyes on him but he had kept out of her way and she had never given him much thought. Could he be out to steal the gold?

A few words with Ban Nolan might be a good idea, decided Nan, and off she went to look for the old woman. She found her standing on an outcrop of rocks behind her cottage. Her layers of skirts were streaming in the wind and her frail body was straining against the fierce gusts. She was gazing out towards Inishbwee.

"The long wait is over, Sorcha Sweeney," she said without looking round. "The spirits of the past have risen at last to do battle with the spirit that is ageless—the spirit of evil."

Nan had always been patient with the old woman. She liked her stories of voices in the night and conversations between ancient gods of sea and sky, but today she felt irritated by such talk. It was no wonder that some people thought that Ban Nolan was astray in the mind and should be in some sort of home for the elderly.

Nevertheless she spoke to the old woman with her usual gentleness. "Ban Nolan," she said softly. "Eimear is over there on the island. Did you tell her something? Something that no one else knows?"

Ban Nolan turned round and fixed Nan with her startling eyes. "Look to your granddaughter, Sorcha Sweeney," she said. "Look to your granddaughter."

Then she turned back to continue her lonely vigil. Nan was now certain that Eimear and the Farrelly children were in dreadful danger.

Nan left Ban Nolan and went to find Mr Farrelly. He was hard to convince that there could possibly be anything to the children's story of Spanish gold but he could see that Nan was worried—very worried indeed.

"Look," he said, "I'll tell you what. I'll go into the post office in Magherabeg and phone Tim Donnelly. He is with the Department of History and Archaeology in the university in Derry. He worked with the teams that discovered those wrecks a few years ago, the *Trinidad Valencero* and the *Girona*, and he helped the museum with the artefacts found on them. If there's any chance of a sunken Spanish galleon or an ounce of gold around Inishbwee, then he's the boy will know. Does that make you feel better?"

"Yes," said Nan. "But I'm coming with you." Mr Farrelly was ages in the phone box. Nan could see him waving his hands about, running his fingers through his hair and scribbling on the back of an envelope. She didn't like the look on his face when he joined her in the car.

"Well?" she said.

"We-l-l," he began. "Tim got very agitated when I

started telling him the story. It seems that for the past few years the university and museum staffs have been researching this area. They have been delving into old documents and studying old maps and all the sorts of things they do in universities, and they came to the conclusion that there was some evidence to suggest that a ship called the *Santa Lucía* may have gone down somewhere around Inishbwee. At the moment they are preparing a major exploration of the seabed, starting at the end of this month. There will be fewer holidaymakers to get in the road. The whole thing is very hush-hush but they had to look for competent divers to help with the work. Of course the divers weren't told what it was all about. Quite a few were interviewed during last winter and one of them was a Mr William Diver. He wasn't taken on because he seemed too anxious to know where exactly the dive would be and what they would be looking for. Tim thinks that he may have gone nosing about until he got some clue about what was going on and decided to go into business for himself. I have to contact the gardaí, and Tim's coming down. He'll be here in a couple of hours."

Nan had been chewing her lip with worry and fear as she listened.

"I'd better make a phone call too," she said and got out of the car and into the phone box. She knew exactly what Eimear's father would have to say when he heard what she had to tell him. Maybe he was right. Maybe she wasn't sensible enough to have her granddaughter to stay for the summer.

"Right," said Mr Farrelly when Nan got back into the car. "Into battle we go! The gardaí first and then we'll

organise a boat—a lifeboat or the coastguards or something—maybe even a helicopter from Finner Camp. The
invasion of Inishbwee is about to begin."

❦ ❦ ❦

13

Life and Death

Kate and Ronan were getting nowhere in their search for Eimear. Kate felt hungrier, colder and tireder than ever before in her whole life.

"We're lost," she said, flinging herself down where a rock and a whin bush met and sheltered her from the wind and rain that stabbed at her face.

"We're not," said Ronan. "Those ruins up there must be Carraig Rua so we are on the Atlantic side of the island. We only have to travel east to get back to the village."

Kate wasn't one little bit comforted. Her nose was already running and now the tears came. She had no hanky so she had to use the sleeve of her anorak. She hated doing that and it made her even more bad-tempered.

"I wish Eimear Kelly had minded her own business," she sniffled. "I hope she's fallen into a hole full of black bogwater and is even colder and wetter than me!"

Kate often said things like this but it was just to get rid

of her anger. She was very kind-hearted really and she was very worried about Eimear.

"Come on," said Ronan. "Maybe we'd better go back to the house and try to light a fi…"

A distant clinking sound caught his attention. "What was that?" he asked.

"What?"

"That noise, like metal hitting stone!"

"I heard nothing," said Kate.

It was nearly impossible to hear anything with the howl of the gale but just then the wind changed direction and they both heard it—clearly if not loudly.

"It's from over there somewhere, behind Carraig Rua," said Ronan excitedly. "Come on. I think we may have found the Black Diver."

Reluctantly, Kate left the comfort of her thorny nest and followed her brother.

The Black Diver had completely removed the topsoil of the mound and had uncovered a layer of small fist-sized stones. These were the stones that Máire MacGinley had gathered to cover the sods she had placed over the dead body of Don Antonio. Eimear thought of the terrific effort that this must have been for the badly wounded young woman.

With a snort of annoyance the man tried to shove the stones aside, but he discovered what Eimear already knew— they had grown into the turf and would not be easily moved. He had to use his spade again.

It was pure torture for Eimear to watch while the Black Diver swore and tore at the stones. She wasn't thinking about what was going to happen to herself; she was thinking of a homesick Spaniard and a brave young Irish woman. Her tears flowed unchecked down her face and sank into the wool of her scarf.

The stones were gone and only the cover of the sods remained. The man took more care now; he didn't want to damage anything precious with the steel of his spade. A grunt of satisfaction told Eimear that he had found what he was looking for and she strained to see, but the man's bulky body was hiding the grave. Then he straightened up and stood aside.

"What do you think of that?" he asked.

Eimear didn't know what she expected to see—a few old bones, perhaps, or maybe nothing but a pile of dust? After all it was a very long time since the burial. What she did see amazed her.

Eimear looked on the face of an old, old man lying at peace. Thin strands of dark hair flowed from the skull to frame that face. The brown leathery skin that covered it was wrinkled and stretched tight over high, delicate cheekbones. More wisps of hair sprouted from the upper lip, which revealed perfectly even but very brown teeth. The eyes were sunken and tightly shut, the hands clasped, locked together for eternity.

"I read about this," said the man. "It's the bog that does it. There's something chemical in the soil that keeps the body from rotting. Your man looks as if he fell asleep under a sun lamp and got a bit fried...Well, this is what I'm interested in."

He poked with his finger at a mouldy pouch which fell

apart and tumbled its contents over the Spaniard's tattered rags of clothes. "They don't look like much now," said the Black Diver, stuffing his pockets with chains and rings and brooches, "but when they're cleaned up and sold to the highest bidder I'll have enough to keep me in strawberries and cream on the Costa del Sol for the rest of my life."

Never had Eimear felt so useless. The man was getting away and she could only sit there and cry.

"Well, I'm off," he said, before he disappeared into the ferns. "Somebody is sure to find you—some time. I hope you don't have as long to wait as His Nibs there."

Eimear sat staring at the face of Don Antonio. Was he blaming her for what had happened? Where was Máire MacGinley? Had she too deserted her? She felt so alone.

Ronan and Kate had followed the clinking sound to the edge of the ferny hollow and soon found the path made by Eimear and the Black Diver. They had crept quietly towards the sounds of digging until they could see the figure bending and straightening as he worked. Then they saw Eimear.

There was nothing they could do to help their friend. Ronan signalled to Kate to creep round in a circle until they could get nearer without being seen. When they had a good view of what was going on, they settled down to wait. Kate thought she would faint when the grave was opened but luckily she couldn't see what was in it.

They watched the Black Diver pocketing his loot and when they were quite sure that he had left the hollow, they crawled out from their hidey-hole.

"Bit tied up, then, at the moment?" grinned Kate, pulling the scarf from Eimear's mouth. Ronan, as always, had a good strong penknife in his pocket and he quickly cut the strings binding her hands and feet. The two girls hugged each other and laughed with relief. Ronan was studying the body in the grave.

"This is fab!" he said. "It's a very important find. Maybe even more important than the treasure."

"The treasure!" exclaimed Eimear. "We mustn't let him get away with it."

And she was off again in hot pursuit of the Black Diver and the stolen treasure. Once she was out of the shelter of the ferny hollow, the full force of the gale hit her. It battered her mercilessly. She fought to stand up against it. Where was the Black Diver? Which direction had he taken? She looked around in panic and Ronan and Kate arrived, panting, at her elbow.

Then she saw it! Away up the hill near Carraig Rua, on the cliffs above the ocean, a huge swirl of seagulls looped and twisted.

"Over there!" she shouted into the wind and once again she had vanished before her two friends had time to draw breath.

"Oh, my God, she's off again!" moaned Ronan. Then he grabbed his sister's hand and tried to follow in Eimear's footsteps.

Again Eimear's feet seemed to be guided over the slippery wet ground. Even the wind was her friend. It came roaring up from the cliff face and curled in behind her, urging her forward. The seagulls were screaming and diving in a frenzy, but only when Eimear had cleared the last of the humps could she see why they were so angry.

The Black Diver was preparing to climb down to the bottom of the cliffs where his rubber dinghy lay secured between two rocks. The gulls were attacking him ferociously, pulling his jacket and dabbing at his eyes. The Black Diver flung his arms up to protect his head but still the birds stabbed at him with their sharp orange beaks. Eimear could see little trails of blood appearing on the man's exposed hands.

Eimear flung herself forward and joined in the battle. She pulled at an arm, screaming as loud as the gulls. "Give it to me! It's not yours! Give it back!"

The Black Diver lashed out, and the force of his blow sent Eimear tumbling to the ground. She reached out and locked both arms around the trousered leg of her enemy and brought him crashing down on top of her. Unable to breathe, she kicked and struggled. At that moment, just below her heart, she felt a sharp scalding pain. It was so intense that for a few seconds she was paralysed. Then, although she was in agony, she forced herself back into the battle. She sank her teeth into the hand that lay across her mouth and the man cursed and rolled away from her towards the edge of the cliff.

He stood up and once again the seagulls descended on him like a swarm of wasps. They gouged at his eyes and tore at his ears. Terrified, the man hit out at them and then he lost his footing on the loose gravelly soil. He fought to keep his balance, waving his arms frantically about. Then, like a scene from a film shot in slow motion, the Black Diver floated off into space, his arms flailing and his jacket ballooning about him. He hung suspended in the air for a fraction of a second, then he disappeared from sight. The look of horror on his face was the last thing Eimear saw before everything went black and she slipped into unconsciousness.

❧ ❧ ❧

14

The Ocean Depths

The scene that greeted Kate as she reached the clifftop was terrifying. She was just in time to see the Black Diver plunge into the depths below and hear the wild scream of despair that tore from his throat. Eimear lay on the ground as pale as death.

Kate rushed over to her and cradled her head on her lap. "Eimear," she called frantically, "are you all right?"

Eimear did not answer and a terrible fear gripped Kate.

"I think she's dead!" she shouted at Ronan. "Oh Eimear, Eimear, please don't be dead!"

She rocked her friend in her arms but not a flicker of life showed on the waxen face.

"There's a boat coming," shouted Ronan. He had climbed up on a higher rock to try to find out what had happened to the Black Diver and had seen, over towards the mainland, the prow of a boat dipping and rising through the huge waves.

"It's going the wrong way!" he exclaimed in frustration. "It's going round to the other side of the island!" He hardly finished the words before going racing off, leaving Kate and Eimear alone.

Kate wasn't even aware that Ronan had left. She was too tortured about Eimear.

"I got them," shouted Ronan, running up towards her and waving something above his head. He had remembered about the flares stored in *Báidín*. He set one off. It rose in an arc in the sky and then dipped gracefully to die in the swell of the ocean. He set off another one.

"They've seen it!" he exulted jumping up and down. "They've changed direction."

Eimear was aware of gentle soothing hands on her body and she opened her eyes. At first she thought she was dreaming. Her mother's anxious face was only inches from her own. Eimear's mother was a nurse and she was looking for broken bones or any other injury that could have caused her daughter such distress. She could find none. "There, there, pet," she crooned when, with relief, she saw Eimear's return to consciousness. "Where is it you hurt?" Eimear wasn't too sure what her mother was talking about. Then she remembered and the pain came stinging again. She gasped and held her ribs. Her mother gently lifted her sweatshirt.

"Is she bad?"

This time it was her father's worried voice Eimear heard.

"I don't know," her mother replied and then she found an angry bruise and continued with relief. "Something very sharp hit her here just below the heart and it has knocked the breath out of her. It might have been the point of a rock when she fell. Anyway, she's all right. She'll be sore for a few days and then she won't be a bit the worse."

It was a miracle! As far as Kate was concerned, Eimear had been dead and now she was alive again. She laughed and cried and then she laughed again. Eimear got slowly to her feet and the party moved down the hill away from the cliffs. There were gardaí everywhere, clumping all over the place in their boots. Ronan was giving directions to his father and a tall thin man who were very carefully carrying something wrapped in a plastic sheet.

"Watch out; the ground's a bit slippery here," he would say or, "Just a little to the right and you're almost there."

A smart boat was riding the waves just offshore. Everything was very confusing. A blanket was wrapped round her shoulders and Eimear was carried through the waves and handed up into the arms of a man in uniform. Other uniformed men were working on a groaning body in the cabin area. She went closer to have a look. It was the Black Diver!

The coastguard heard her sharp intake of breath and he turned round. "It's Ok, darlin'," he said. "This bag of pus can do you no harm at all now."

"Is he badly hurt?" asked Eimear.

"Not bad enough," wheezed the man. He was helping to hold a leg straight as another man fitted a splint. "A broken leg, some busted ribs and a nice bloody cut down his cheek. We'll have him fit for the courtroom in a few weeks.

We picked him out of the water at the bottom of the cliffs. He's a very lucky man the tide was in." On a bench to the side of the Black Diver lay the pile of dull, dirty metal.

"Thank God you're safe!" Nan Sweeney's normally calm face was twisted with anxiety and streaked with tears. "You must be starved," she said, setting Eimear down in a sheltered spot and opening her picnic-basket. A steaming mug of Nan's chicken broth was placed firmly in Eimear's hand and the delicious smell of it sent her stomach wild with joy. She sipped gratefully and snuggled up against the two women who loved her most in all the world.

"Carefully now, careful."

Mr Farrelly, her father and the tall thin man were manoeuvring the plastic-sheeted bundle into the coast-guard boat. Mr Farrelly called the thin man Tim: so Eimear guessed they were old friends.

"Good," said Tim Donnelly when he saw that the bundle was safely settled on a bench. He wrapped two cords round it and tied it safely to the side of the boat.

"Would you not have been better to have left it where it was and get the experts to come and collect it?" asked Ronan.

"Indeed not," answered Tim, huffed a little at not being considered an expert. "Once the air gets at the body it has to be removed to museum conditions immediately. If we left it any longer it would begin to deteriorate. I will ring the museum from Magherabeg and let them know of this new development. They will make the proper arrange-ments."

"You're going to be famous, my girl," he said, addressing Eimear. "A treasure trove *and* a sixteenth-century body. The museum authorities will be delighted."

Everybody was on board now: Ronan and Kate, Mr Farrelly, her own mammy and daddy and the four gardaí.

"Well, what do you think of young Miss Kelly, then?" her father asked of the whole assembly. Eimear was surprised at the tone of his voice. "The Kellys always had good heads in a crisis." He reached over and patted Eimear's knee. The pride was just bursting out of him.

The powerful engines of the boat started and it ploughed through the buffeting waves with barely a bump. Two great big blades of water fanned out behind them. From the cliffs below Carraig Rua the seagulls rose. Flying as if they were a single body, they swooped and swirled and settled to circle above the boat. This time there was no anger in their plaintive calls. Their cries were of mourning, of loneliness, of lands far away across the western ocean, of souls lost and wandering.

"Noisy wee divils," shouted a fat garda to Eimear when he saw her concern. "They think we're a fishing boat and might be throwing out a few heads and a parcel of guts."

Eimear nodded but she didn't answer and the garda turned his attention to Kate, who was sitting beside him enjoying his jokes. Nan's picnic basket was open at her feet and Eimear could see the glint of Nan's sharp kitchen knife.

When she was sure no one was looking, she slipped the knife up under her blanket. As soon as they reached the deepest part of the water she slid along her seat until she was beside the bundle in the plastic sheeting. Under cover of her blanket, she hooked the blade under the first cord and sliced through it. She did the same with the second. Everybody was so busy talking about the frights they had had and what a great success the day had been that nobody paid any attention to Eimear at all.

There wasn't any means of hiding what she was going to do next. So she just stood up, eased her hands under the bundle and lifted. Don Antonio's body was no weight at all. There was little left of him but a few fragile bones held together by the leathery skin. Slowly and with reverence she raised Don Antonio high in the air and said, "I return you to the waters, Don Antonio de Serralles. May your soul rest in peace among friends."

Then she dropped the bundle into the hungry waves.

The seagulls rose up and their cry now was joyous. It swelled and grew into a wild chorus of celebration that drowned out the howling of the gale. The triumphant sea-birds circled for a few seconds round the spot where the body of Don Antonio had disappeared. Then, as one, they swerved slowly and gracefully and turned towards the western ocean.

❦ ❦ ❦

15

Fuss and Forgiveness

There was a horrified silence for a few moments after Eimear's dramatic burial at sea and then everyone on board began to speak at once. Tim Donnelly rushed to the side and ordered the boat to turn round, but the parcel in the plastic sheeting had completely disappeared.

"It was invaluable," he stammered, mad with frustration. "Why did you do such a stupid thing?"

"Hold on, Tim," said Eimear's dad. "She didn't know what she was doing. She's had a bad shock and she's not out of it yet."

"Put a marker down," ordered Tim Donnelly. "Maybe the divers will be able to recover it."

Eimear smiled to herself. The divers would find nothing. She watched the gulls until they became a blur on the horizon and then they disappeared. Don Antonio would never return home but at least he was safe with the souls of his friends and would find rest in that mysterious land lost in the mists of the western ocean.

"What do I tell the museum?" said Tim Donnelly, with a worried look in his face.

"Nothing," said Mr Farrelly. "Sure you didn't tell them anything about a body, did you? I knew nothing about it when I phoned you. Even the guards don't know what was in that parcel."

"You're right," agreed Tim. "All the same, I think I ought to report it."

"Do whatever you think best," said Eimear's dad. "But you have a hoard of Spanish gold to bring back. That should make you a very important person in the museum's eyes."

"I suppose so," agreed Tim Donnelly reluctantly.

On the shore below Nan's house all the neighbours had gathered. Sending for the coastguards is an occasion not to be missed around Magherabeg. When the boat neared the beach, Bran, Aonghas and Rory leapt into the water barking excitedly and, much as their mother tried to restrain them, the Farrelly twins followed. The poor woman had to let them go: she had her arms full of baby. The excitement was great! Everyone trooped up the steps after the players in the drama, and garbled versions of the story went from listener to listener.

Every little scrap of information was gathered and stored. Letters would be written to loved ones in America and England and this extra bit of gossip would add a touch of spice. Eimear, Kate and Ronan were hurried off for hot baths and a change of clothes. The coastguards had radioed for an ambulance and the Black Diver was carried in a stretcher up the steep steps and then whisked off to Letterkenny hospital. A stiff-faced garda went with him.

"That bruise has gone!" exclaimed Eimear's mother in astonishment. She was bringing fresh towels to Eimear, who was lying stretched in the warm, steamy waters of Nan's huge bath and thoroughly enjoying herself.

"It's impossible!" continued her mother. "A bruise that size doesn't disappear in an hour. I know I saw it. I didn't imagine it."

Eimear just smiled and scooted some water at her mother. How could she explain that the pain that had seared through her was the pain of the knife-wound that had led to the death of a young woman far back in the mists of time?

Mrs Kelly wasn't one to brood too long about things she didn't understand so she splashed her daughter in return and set about washing her hair. What had become of the bruise was a mystery she couldn't explain but she was grateful that there was now no sign of the injury.

Out in Nan's kitchen it was all go. Tim Donnelly had got in touch with the museum in Dublin and arranged for a security van to transport the gold and jewellery. An expert would be on hand immediately to advise on cleaning and restoration work. They would eventually make a press announcement, but in the meantime the whole business would be kept quiet. Mr Kelly was taking great delight in examining the jewelled ornaments and chains of all sizes.

"Just imagine what it will look like when it is all cleaned up," he said, balancing a little dagger in his hand. "How much do you think it is all worth?"

"Stuff like that is priceless really," answered Tim Donnelly. "If William Diver had managed to get away with it the word would have gone around among the wealthiest collectors in the world and it would have been sold for the Lord knows how many millions."

"But the people who bought it—what could they have done with it?" asked Mrs Kelly as she passed through on the way to the washhouse with Eimear's dirty clothes. "They could hardly wear it, could they? If it was put on show at all sure they'd be charged with receiving stolen goods."

"Exactly right," said Tim. "Those people just keep treasures for their own private viewing. Sometimes they don't even look at them. They're locked up in a vault somewhere and are never seen again. I don't believe those people are even interested in the beauty of the objects. They just want to know they own them. It makes them feel secure—secure and wealthy and powerful. At least now the gold will belong to all the Irish people and will be on view for them to see any time they want."

"There'll be some compensation for Eimear too, you know," continued Tim. "She was the one who found it."

"I didn't know that," said Eimear, her voice muffled by a towel as she stood at the bathroom door.

"Oh, yes," nodded Tim. "It won't be anywhere near the real value of the treasure, of course, but it will be a good sum. Quite a few thousand, I would guess."

"Well, what do you think of that, Eimear?" said her dad, grinning at her. "What are you going to do with all that nice money?"

Eimear thought for a while and then she said, "The three of us found the gold, Kate, Ronan and me. So if there is comp...comp...a reward, then we get equal shares. But I know what I want to do. I want to travel. I'll go to Spain. I'd like to visit Valencia."

Eimear went to bed early that night and she slept soundly until her Nan rattled the bedroom door and brought in her breakfast on a tray. The tray was decorated with flowers from the garden and Nan had made Eimear's favourite wheaten scones, burning them slightly round the edges the way she liked them.

"Thank God to see you sitting there and so well at yourself," said Nan Sweeney, sitting on the edge of the bed and smiling as Eimear piled slabs of yellow butter and heaps of rhubarb jam on the scones. "You gave me an awful fright; you know that, don't you, Eimear?"

Eimear's hand stopped half way to her mouth and she looked at her Nan. She felt very guilty. Poor Nan must have been out of her mind with worry. "I'm sorry, Nan," she said. "I could think of nothing else but stopping the Black Diver."

"Well, you certainly did that," replied Nan, and then she laughed. "You should have heard your daddy when I phoned to tell him what you were up to."

"Don't tell me," said Eimear and she did a good imitation of her father's voice. "There you are! You see? What did I say would happen if she kept going to Magherabeg? Nobody listens to me but I have an awful habit of being right. The Sweeneys are all daft. It's in the blood. Didn't I say that?"

Nan was rocking round the bed with laughter.

"And then did you see the pride of him when you saved the gold?" she cackled.

"Ah," smiled Eimear, "but that was my Kelly side

coming out."

"Go on, eat your breakfast," laughed Nan. "I think we're both forgiven—this time."

Eimear didn't need a second invitation.

"I'm glad Ronan at least had the wit to leave a note," said Nan as she went out the door. "If he hadn't, I wonder how it would all have turned out?"

Eimear had to admit that Nan was right and she was glad that Ronan hadn't listened to her when they were leaving the cottage.

🐞 🐞 🐞

16

The Gold Cross of Inishbwee

The weather had changed completely again, as it frequently does in Donegal, and the sun was streaming down over a calm blue sea.

"Come on for a swim," shouted Kate to Eimear from the door of the caravan.

"I will," answered Eimear. "I'm dying for a dip but I have something to do first. You and Ronan go on down. I'll be there in about ten minutes."

Ban Nolan's cottage lay soaking up the sun. The steam was rising from the black slates on the roof and from the drooping thatch on the outhouse. The old woman was snoozing in her chair when Eimear peeped through the open door. She looked very old and very, very frail. The blue eyes opened immediately though Eimear had made no sound.

"Come in, Eimear," the soft voice whispered. "Sit down beside me."

Eimear sat on the three-legged stool in front of Ban Nolan's chair and the old woman looked at her with her strange eyes; eyes she had seen in the picture on the wall and under the woollen blanket of a young woman on Inishbwee.

"A lot has happened since you were here last, Eimear Kelly. A lot that most people wouldn't understand."

Eimear nodded. She knew she didn't have to tell Ban Nolan about her doings on Inishbwee.

"Now my poor body and my poor soul can be at rest. The promise has been kept. I have had a good long life on this earth. The time is near when I will go to start a new life in another place."

Although she knew Ban Nolan was talking about her own death, Eimear didn't feel sad, because Ban Nolan wasn't sad. She was smiling happily as if some special treat that she had been looking forward to for ages was about to happen.

"I have something for you, Eimear," she said and she reached up under her jacket and produced a blue leather box with designs in gold around the edges. It was about four inches square and two deep. The leather was scuffed and the gold worn thin in places. "Don't open it until you are by yourself. May it always remind you of the old woman of the island and the day on Inishbwee when you fulfilled an ancient vow."

Eimear carried the box carefully until she reached the sanctuary of her bedroom. There was no one about. She could hear the happy squeals of the Farrellys on the beach and the clink of Nan's spade as she worked in her vegetable patch. Her parents and Tim Donnelly had gone back two days before and things had returned to normal.

There were two little brass catches on the box and Eimear's fingers trembled a she eased them open one by one. Her heart was dancing a jig as she lifted the lid. A piece of thick parchment lay on top of the contents and Eimear lifted it out. There, on a bed of white satin, lay a beautiful cross—the Golden Cross of Inishbwee!

Carefully Eimear carried it over to the window to get a better look at it. The cross she had seen in the photograph in Ban Nolan's house, the cross that been a christening present four hundred years ago, glinted and shone in the bright sunlight. In the centre glowed a fiery red jewel and on each arm of the cross a stone of deepest blue lay embedded in a pool of gold.

Suddenly Eimear remembered the paper she had tossed so carelessly aside. Curiosity drew her back to the bed and she unfolded the stiff paper. There were actually two sheets of paper. One was a document of some kind, for it was written on official paper with a solicitor's name on the heading and a stamp at the bottom. It was proof that the cross belonged to Nóirín MacGinley and was hers to dispose of as she wished.

At first Eimear was puzzled but then she realised that Nóirín McGinley was Ban Nolan's real name! She looked then at the second piece of paper and was astonished to see that it was a sort of family tree. It traced all the female descendants of Caitlín MacSweeney, Máire MacGinley and her daughter María right down to the present day. There were MacFaddens and O'Donnells and MacGinleys and

MacSweeneys galore, for all of the women had changed their names on marriage. Eimear was surprised to see that her own great-grandmother was Ban Nolan's first cousin.

With a stab of excitement Eimear saw that beside one name in each generation a little cross had been drawn. There was a cross beside Ban Nolan's name and there was one beside another name, the very last on the tree. There it was: her own name, Eimear Kelly, scrawled in spidery writing and beside it the little cross.

At the bottom of the page the same spidery writing declared the same Eimear Kelly to be the new owner of the Cross of Inishbwee. It was signed by Nóirín MacGinley and witnessed by Ned Crossan the postman. Poor Ned had probably thought Ban Nolan was away in the head but he signed her paper to keep her happy.

Eimear clutched the cross tight against her body. Never had she felt so honoured! This was the cross that had come all the way from Spain and had been given to Máire MacGinley's daughter at her christening! She would treasure it for ever.

❦ ❦ ❦

17

The Eimear Collection

Secrets are very hard to keep in Ireland, as there is nothing people like better than a good story. So a few weeks later the papers were full of rumours about a huge hoard of Spanish gold being found in Donegal on the island of Inishbwee.

People came by the car-load and the bus-load to get a look at the island and many hired boats to do a bit of treasure-seeking themselves. The gardaí and the coast-guards were fed up patrolling the waters and keeping tresspassers from digging all over the island.

The university and the museum authorities were worried that their expedition to search for the sunken *Santa Lucía* was now at risk and so they decided to hold a press conference earlier than they had planned.

Eimear, Kate and Ronan were taken to Dublin to the National Museum and, dressed in their Sunday best, they had to face the questions and the cameras. The director of the museum showed them into a huge room, the walls of which, weighed down with massive paintings, soared high above their heads to meet an elaborately decorated ceiling. In the centre of the room was a brilliantly polished table and to the side of the table was a glass case draped in a blue silk cloth. There were several important officials in the room but the most important of all was the Spanish ambassador, who would perform the unveiling ceremony.

The television cameras and the journalists were ranged in front of the table and the camera lights almost blinded the children until they got used to them. As usual Nan Sweeney stole the show. She was decked out in a bright scarlet dress with layers of frills that bounced around her dimpled knees. On her head was a black lace mantilla held in place by a beautiful mother-of-pearl comb, and huge brass curtain rings dangled from her ears. There were flowers in her hair and flowers behind both ears. She furled and unfurled a homemade fan that she had painted and decorated herself. The evening was in honour of the Spanish nation and she felt it was only polite to dress properly for the occasion.

Eimear's father was not amused. "That crazy woman," he growled when he was poked in the eye by the fan for the second time. "Would you just look at her? She has no shame. Wouldn't she disgrace you? Let's hope they don't unveil her instead of the gold!"

But the journalists loved Nan. They flashed their cameras and called out to her for special poses. Nan smilingly obliged and Mr Kelly seethed. The Spanish ambassador, too, took a shine to Nan and when the director finally got everybody seated at the table he placed Eimear, Kate and Ronan on one side and the ambassador, Nan Sweeney and Mrs Kelly on the other. There was just room for Mr Kelly to squeeze in at the end of the table but unfortunately he was out of range of the television cameras.

The director opened the news conference by welcoming his guests and then giving brief details of where the hoard had been discovered. Then he allowed the journalists to ask questions. Eimear was now the centre of attention. Each reporter stood up, gave their name and the name of the paper they worked for.

"Laura Higgins, *Irish Times*. Could you tell us, Eimear, exactly how you found the gold?"

This was the question Eimear had been dreading and she had been torturing her brain trying to find an answer that would be believable. She was certainly not going to say that a four-hundred-year-old ghost had led her to the treasure!

"Well," she said hesitantly, "I...ah...I just...sort of...tripped over it."

This reply didn't seem to satisfy the reporters and a barrage of questions was flung at her, but she pretended to be shy and a bit dazed by it all and kept repeating her original answer.

The questions then turned to the part played by the Black Diver in the affair. Here the director intervened and stated that as William Diver was awaiting trial it would not be proper to discuss his actions. To Eimear's relief, no mention was made of the body found on the island. No one seemed to know about it, not even the director.

There were many queries about the possibility of more gold being found on Inishbwee but the director declared this to be most unlikely.

"From our research we have reason to believe that the *Santa Lucía* went to the bottom with all the crew and all their goods on board. How the gold came to be on the island is a mystery but it seems likely that the captain may have flung his pouch onto the land just before the ship went under. Someone on the island found it and buried it. There is no more gold to be found on Inishbwee."

By this time the director had decided that the questions had gone on long enough and he called on the Spanish ambassador to remove the blue silk cloth.

"Ladies and gentlemen," said the ambassador as he stood beside the glass case, holding Eimear firmly by the hand, "it gives me great pleasure to reveal to the world the beauty that was created in my own country so long ago and which was discovered by this young lady on a windswept island in Donegal."

With a dramatic flourish he removed the silk sheet from the glass case.

There were sharp intakes of breath from the audience, followed by flurries of flashes. The hoard was smaller than the rumours had led them to expect, but they were unprepared for its magnificence. Even Eimear was stunned. The long chains cascaded like golden waterfalls over folds of rich red velvet, and the coloured stones in the jewelled rings and brooches glowed and sparkled as if they were brand-new. The little dagger lay in the centre, a credit to the Spanish goldsmith who had lovingly designed it centuries ago. A card written in beautiful lettering and propped at the front of the case announced to the the world,

The Eimear Collection.

Discovered on Inishbwee Island, Co.Donegal, 1992, by Eimear Kelly, Kate Farrelly and Ronan Farrelly.

Back home in Derry, Eimear was a VIP for a time. Her school did a project on the Spanish Armada and she had to go from class to class telling her story and showing pictures of the Eimear Collection. Her friends were more interested in hearing about her television appearance, but when they learned that she hadn't met anybody really famous their interest soon waned. After a while the fuss died down and things got back to normal.

The weather was good that autumn and the team from the university continued to dive around Inishbwee right up until the end of October, but nothing was found. About that time, the Black Diver was charged with the attempted theft of national treasures and was fined a hefty sum. The guards wanted to add assault to his list of crimes but neither Eimear nor her parents wished to press charges. The man had such a scare when he fell off the cliff that they were sure he would never go treasure-hunting again.

Just after Christmas, Nan Sweeney wrote to say that Ban Nolan had died peacefully in her sleep and had been buried on her beloved Inishbwee. Eimear was a bit sad at first but then she remembered the happy look on the old woman's face when she talked about going to a new life. She would visit her grave in the summer and bring an armful of flowers from Nan's garden.

There will be many more summers in Magherabeg and Eimear thinks that nothing will change there. She forgets of course that people change. When she grows up her eyes may no longer see what it was about Magherabeg that made her holidays there so magical. She *has* something that will always remind her of one summer in particular. The scuffed blue leather box with the worn designs is locked in a drawer in a bank. It will stay there until she is eighteen and then she will take it out. Some day, if she has a daughter, she will pass it on to her and she is glad that the promise made four hundred years ago by Máire MacGinley has been kept. Her daughter will read this story and she will be proud to own the Gold Cross of Inishbwee.

Also by Poolbeg

The Hiring Fair

By

Elizabeth O'Hara

It is 1890 and Parnell is the uncrowned king of
Ireland. But thirteen-year-old Sally Gallagher,
"Scatterbrain Sally" as her mother and young
sister Katie call her, has no interest in politics.
She is happy to read books and leave the
running of the house to those who like house-
work.

A shocking tragedy changes the lives of the
sisters. Instead of being the daughters of a
comfortable Donegal farmer and fisherman,
they have to become hired servants, bound for
six months to masters they don't know.

Elizabeth O'Hara has written an exciting
story that has its share of sorrow and joy. She
creates in Scatterbrain Sally a new and
unforgettable Irish heroine.

Also by Poolbeg

World Myths & Tales

By

Carolyn Swift

This is a collection of twelve mythological tales, from places as far afield as India, China, Japan, Australia, New Zealand, Canada, North, South and Central America, Persia, Egypt and Black Africa. Appropriately, in this "Year of Indigenous Peoples", there are myths of the Maoris, the Aborigines, the Basutos, the Canarians and the North American Passamaquoddy tribe.

Dragons, giants and a variety of monsters figure in many of these tales, but there are also stories of evil and ambitious kings, independent-minded women and mischievious boys, as well as of remarkable animals and birds, from snakes and giant lizards to llamas and parrots. Several creation myths are included, which tell of the lighting up of the sun, the shaping of the world and of how people escaped the great flood.

Also by Poolbeg

The First Christmas

By

Michael Mullen

Daniel is ten and loves Christmas. He is a great friend of John Duffy, the local carpenter who carves the figures for the village crib.

One night before Christmas Daniel steps inside the crib and finds himself in Bethlehem just before the birth of the Christ child. He meets the shepherds and the Magi and is placed in mortal danger by Herod's murdering soldiers...

Michael Mullen has retold the world's best-known story with humour, freshness and excitement.